RUTH SKILBECK
THE GIRLS AND THE GHOSTS OF THE OLD MANSE REVISITED

AN AUSTRALIAN FUGUE NOVEL

BORDERSTREAM BOOKS

The Girls and the Ghosts of The Old Manse Revisited
An Australian Fugue Novel

First Edition; Series Edition
Published in 2025
Published by Borderstream Books
PO Box 124, Newcomb, VIC 3219, Australia
www.borderstreambooks.com.au

A catalogue record for this book is available from the National Library of Australia

ISBN: 9780645194135 (paperback)

THE GIRLS AND THE GHOSTS OF THE OLD MANSE REVISITED

Ruth Skilbeck is a British-Australian author with Irish ancestry. Her books include her Australian Fugue novels *The Antipode Room* and *Sayonara Baby,* and *The Writer's Fugue: Musicalization, Trauma and Subjectivity in the Literature of Modernity* based on her Doctor of Philosophy thesis (University of Technology Sydney). In addition to her PhD, she holds a Master of Arts in Writing, and a Graduate Certificate in Higher Education Teaching and Learning all from University of Technology Sydney, and a Bachelor of Arts with Honours in Philosophy, from Birkbeck, University of London. She worked as a freelance journalist in Dublin, London, and Sydney, specialising in arts writing, and lectured in journalism writing subjects at universities including University of Technology Sydney, and the University of New South Wales. She is an author of journal articles, stories, poetry, essays, and book talks (in her youth as writer-and-presenter for BBC World Service Radio's Book Choice). Her writings are published in books, journals, magazines and newspapers from peer reviewed publications such as a chapter in *Cultural Studies of Rights: Critical Articulations* (Routledge); articles in *Pacific Journalism Review*; essays and articles in *The Irish Times* and *Sunday Tribune,* and *Australian Art Review*; she was awarded a PhD scholarship and several grants (including the Australia Council New Work for visual arts writing). She is founding editor-in-chief of *Escape Artists Anthology* and *Arts Features International* anthology journal.

Books by Ruth Skilbeck include:

The Australian Fugue Series of standalone novels
The Antipode Room (illustrated with photographic art)
Missing (abridged edition of *The Antipode Room*)
Sayonara Baby (also published as *Cafe Life in the Antipodes*)
The Girls and the Ghosts of The Old Manse Revisited

Related works
Sayonara Baby-Fragments of Memory Images (photographic art images and brief excerpts from Australian Fugue novels)

Musico-literary studies (PhD thesis and revised book)
The Writer's Fugue: Musicalization, Trauma and Subjectivity in the Literature of Modernity

Anthology and Journal
Escape Artists Anthology editor-in-chief
Arts Features International editor-in-chief

Contents

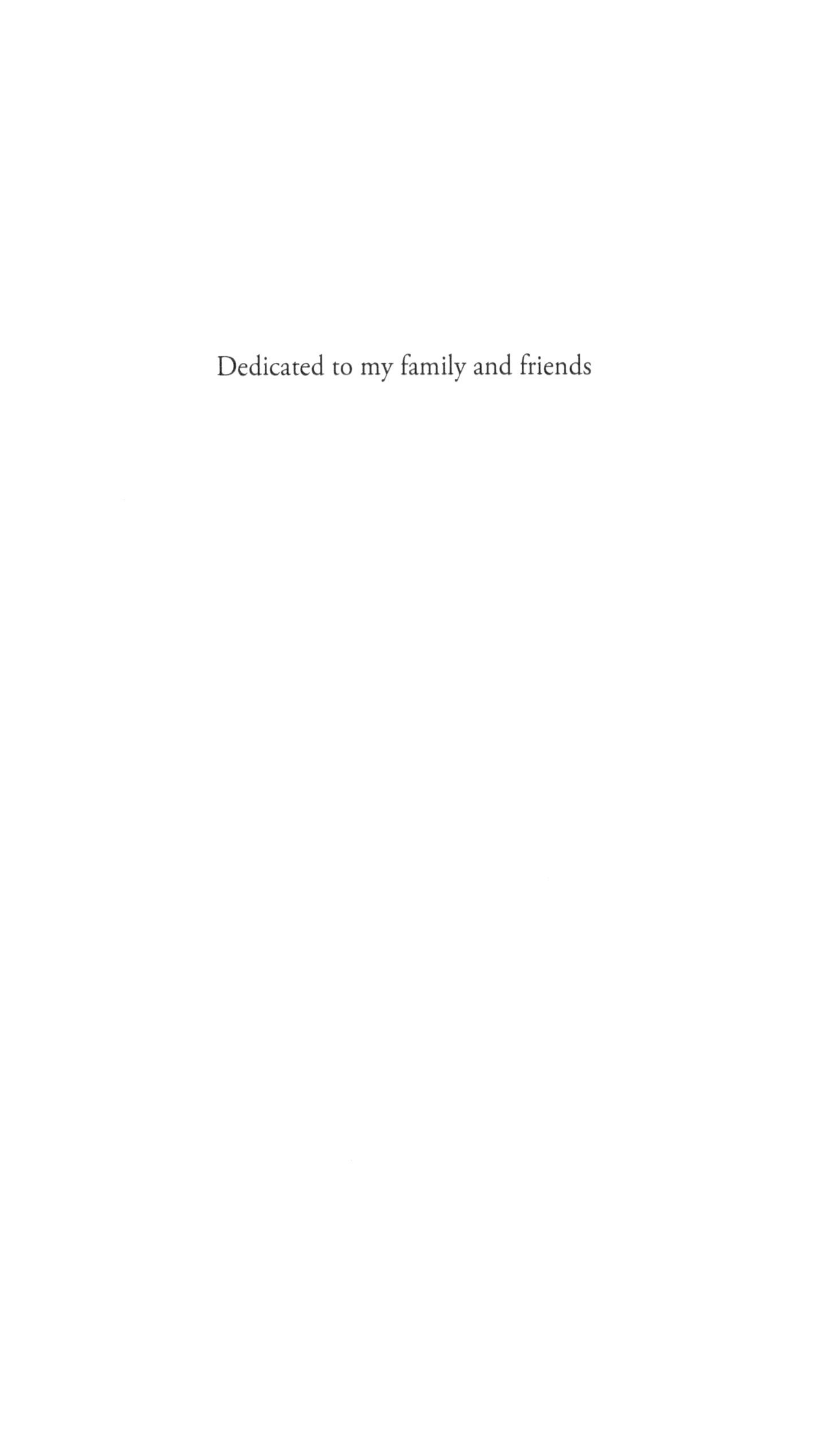

Dedicated to my family and friends

THE HOUSE OF GHOSTS

We were all ghosts. My mother in the kitchen. My friends; the Seven. My little brother in the TV room. The smiling woman from the cottages who came to clean. And the others. Restlessly flitting around our little underworld.

And me I was the most restless ghost of all, in, out, as the seasons played over the Glens and the Causeway Coast.

Sometimes, when I close my eyes or when I sleep, it's as if the house is still inside me. I have dreamt the house so often, I wonder, can you be haunted by a house? Dreams like a long running series, each one conjuring a graphic development of the ones before. Each one ends abruptly, without ending. As I wake up struggling for breath.

I'm on the ground floor. The big house is empty, an echoing shell of shadows towering above me. But I can feel the ghost. Inside me, electrocuting every pore with fear. I can feel the ghost in the air, hollow as death. I start to float up and up just above the staircase. I cannot stop myself floating towards the ghost. Her presence is becoming stronger and more powerful. Fighting terror, I ascend towards the third storey. The top of the house is her lair. (Why is it always a "she"? I wonder now). I am drawn upwards into the attic. A swirling fog of energies, a forcefield of horror zaps towards me. The ghost is invisible.

Our psychic energies inter-lock. For a nightmarish moment, I am overcome. Frozen. Lost. The sense of evil she generates is thick and overpowering. Then I rally. I gather all my courage.

This is it. This time can I do it. The purpose of the dream is always the same. By using a supreme effort of will, summoning up all my strength, I must vanquish my paralysing fear. Like a comic book superhero, I must overcome the ghost, to save the world, and save myself.

PART ONE

ROXANNE

Northern Ireland. Europe
1972-1975

1

ARRIVAL AT THE OLD MANSE

Winter-Spring 1972

The Old Manse was an imposing Georgian nineteenth-century manor, situated in a river glen in County Antrim farmland. After lying empty for longer than people could remember, the house had recently been rescued and restored. Painted yellow, with black paint outlining its windows and the lamp-flanked portal of its front door. I could see it from miles away, as we approached in Bertie, our van, along the narrow road which ran along the ridge.

Few buildings were scattered among the fields and peat bog in the valley–just the occasional farmhouse. The yellow house stood out like a landmark. The largest residence in the parish, alone on a rise above a river, it drew the eyes of passing travellers, namely, on that winter's day, myself and my family.

What I could see from the van, embellished by memory, was a drive lined with towering rhododendron bushes that led to the house. Fields spread to the front and side, fenced off from a neighbouring farm. I could just see a high stone-walled stable yard behind the house, beyond it, a walled garden, and an old dry well. At the back of the property, I would discover too was a lofty stand of beech trees that was home to a screeching murder of crows. The house faced a mountain on the horizon. The back windows looked out over a downhill incline levelling to pasture bordering a silver-green river meandering peacefully through steep riverbanks.

It was a dull grey February afternoon when first I set eyes on the house. My family had moved to Northern Ireland seven weeks before, my father had been appointed to a professorial chair, his first, at the local university. We had arrived from England, and were renting accommodation in town while we looked for our next home. For what seemed like forever, every weekend we'd climbed into Bertie, our cream-coloured van, and set off house-hunting.

We had been shown around several large, vacated houses in the countryside. The Old Manse was the latest property on the list. I thought all the places we'd seen were unsettling. We'd walked through a derelict mansion, and a farmhouse filled with dust and shadows, and the indistinct memories of other people's lives. I didn't say anything, but the houses gave me the creeps. It troubled me that I felt this way.

As I walked around the echoing corridors and outbuildings of one empty place after another, I tried to hide my apprehension. I was the eldest, I was almost thirteen (less than six months to go) and I had to be brave.

"That must be it! There it is!" Dad announced in the jovial tone he used when he wanted everyone to please cheer up. He'd lifted his hand and pointed. The house stood out like a lighthouse on a cliff.

"Really?" my mother said. "Do you really think so?"

"Well, there isn't anything else," replied my father.

The road was flanked with verges and hawthorn hedgerows. I'd never seen such long green grass. We drove past a ruined church. Dad spun the steering wheel and the van turned at a sharp right angle into an even narrower road.

"The Lane," he said with a chuckle. We were deep in arable farming country, we passed fallow fields, and cows in pasture, and the miasma of grass, leaves and vegetation on either side of the lane made me feel almost nauseous, as if I was underwater holding my breath. I gazed out of the car window towards the approaching house.

As it turned out, I needn't have worried about dereliction, or standards of interior design. Its owners were Roscoe Golightly, film actor, and his partner, Coralie Kott, film actor. Roscoe told our family he had discovered the house when he was driving through the countryside. It had been dilapidated and derelict, used to store tools by the local farmer. Now, the dining room walls were clad with cork. In the bathroom, mirror tiles backed a spa bath, the floor was tiled with marble. The house was warm, thanks to the oil-fuelled central heating.

There was a TV room on the top floor to the approval of us younger people. This room, devoted to lounging, had a brown and white tiled floor and yellow walls. An antique *chaise longue* refreshed in burgundy velvet upholstery, floor cushions and bean bags tempted viewing sloth opposite the biggest colour TV I had seen. This was destined to be left behind. Roscoe, who we warmed to, had a talk with my father, with whom he shared a taste for Indian guru shirts. Dad was tall, he had fair hair, a calm confident manner, and charisma. He had taken to wearing a kurta when working in India and had brought back several that he wore at home. But he was sporting a light grey suit with a shirt and tie that day. It was Roscoe who was wearing a mid length embroidered turquoise kurta, jeans, and a beige tunic jacket.

My mother, medium height, with black hair that she always wore up, was wearing an Indian silk scarf my father had given her, and a sand-coloured raincoat over her green skirt suit. My parents were from Australia, the distant country on the other side of the world that Lily, Alex, and I had visited with Mum before Sarah came along. When I was growing up I lost count of how many times people (men) who were basically strangers said to me, if you get a spade and start digging, you'll end up there.

The thing Roscoe said that stuck in my mind as he showed us around that first time was that this was a "marching area." Once a year in summer there were marches of pipes and drum bands, there were practices on the local roads for weeks ahead, the music could be heard from miles around, of a drum that was made not far from here. "It's quite primal," he said. "But there might not be marches this year. They are banned."

"Because of Bloody Sunday, the massacre at the civil rights march in January, last month, lots of unarmed marchers were killed," said my little brother Alex, age nine.

We all looked at him in surprise.

"I hear about it on the news." Alex said.

"We're not talking about that Alex," said my father.

My father told us that Roscoe told him he liked our family, he wanted the house he loved to go to us; he knew we'd cherish it just as he had. And he had suggested a price so astonishingly low my parents could afford it, as, although they didn't tell us, Roscoe and Coralie wanted to leave as soon as they could; it was almost impossible to sell a house like it in the Troubles.

Six weeks later we moved in, with Dusty our Labrador dog, and Jester our cat, and shortly after that the three stables were filled with ponies and a donkey; two goats inherited along with two cats from Roscoe and Coralie, and twenty-two hens who laid an egg each (almost) every day. The next year my mother would give the excess eggs to a butcher in the nearest town and he sold them in his shop. In return, he would fill up Mum's car boot with sacks stinking and sodden with the hearts of freshly slaughtered cows, which she would cut up in the kitchen for Dusty. (It made naked, raw and literal the economy of animal feeding, killing animals to feed animals, that I, a vegetarian by choice because I loved animals and did not wish to eat them, found disturbing). But that was in the future.

2

THE GHOSTS, 1972

And then we learned about the ghosts. During the waiting-time for the sale to be finalised and for Coralie and Roscoe to move out of the house, I accompanied Dad on visits to the place to plant trees. Coralie suggested that I might help look after her horses, and horse-mad girl that I was, I felt privileged to be invited and more than happy to.

One chilly March afternoon all us went to The Old Manse, to help Dad with the tree planting. Half a dozen silver birch saplings had been successfully dug into the earth and we were standing around in the downstairs hallway of the house with the actors. Then Roscoe Golightly said:

"You know there's a ghost in the house. She's hanging on the upper-floor landing!"

There was a startled silence as we all looked at him.

"With her husband!" Coralie added.

"Really?" my mother said, in a sceptical tone.

Our expressions of incomprehension, disquiet and surprise provoked the householders' mirth, as they laughed together.

"They're in the old photographs on the upper landing in the stairwell. The Minister and his wife. They were the last ones who lived here before the house was abandoned. I'll show you if you'd like to follow me upstairs?"

"Yes," I said.

"Well alright," said my father. And we trooped towards the staircase.

"It's an interesting story," Roscoe continued enthusiastically as he walked, as if he thought every self-respecting old Irish country manor should have its ghost and ghost stories, as if it was all part of the appeal, but an unreceptive chill was emanating from some of his audience. Namely my parents. "Well, here we are, here they are!" said Roscoe waiting for us all to join him, crowding onto the landing on the staircase. We all turned our eyes towards the portraits on the wall.

"They lived in the house for many years. They had children, but they all died here in the house. That's why they moved out and the manse became derelict," Roscoe continued theatrically, lowering his voice with dramatic emphasis.

I nodded, less than thrilled to hear this. It was a disturbing and tragic story about what had now been revealed to be a disturbing house.

After we walked back downstairs, it was Coralie's turn to tell us all a story, recounting a terrifying incident which had happened to her in the house. Roscoe had accepted a one-year contract to make a TV series in America. He filmed in blocks of weeks, then had time off when he flew back to see her. This meant that Coralie was left alone in the house for weeks at a time.

One night, Roscoe was in America and Coralie was home on her own, reading in bed.

She heard a car driving up the driveway, towards the house.

Coralie heard it driving erratically, swerving, and screeching tyres burning the long rhododendron drive. It had come right up to the turning circle. Horn blowing; men's voices yelling and shouting. She peeked out through a crack in the curtains. The car drove around, menacingly, headlights splashing across foliage. Terrified, she tried to barricade herself in the bedroom with its four-poster bed, she pushed a dressing table and chairs against the doors and rang the police from the telephone on the bedside antique table.

The shouting and whooping were growing more frenzied. She could hear men's loud voices. They must have got out of the car. They were shouting threats and obscenities.

"We're going to get you!" "We're breaking in now!" "We're in the house!"

"We're going to rape you!"

She was so scared she couldn't move. She was frozen under her handmade quilt.

She was sure she heard a window breaking. She thought: They're in the house! Time stretched into an eternity of terror. Where were the police? She rang again, hardly able to speak with fear,

"Please come now, I can hear them, I think they've broken into the house!"

After what seemed like forever the car drove away. Roscoe took over the tale: "The police, who were based in the village, turned up hours after Coralie made her desperate phone call. After taking her statement they told her there was nothing they could do. But to let them know if anything else happened."

That solved the mini-mystery of why they were selling their beloved old manse, after only two years of living here.

It was haunted and trespassed upon; it wasn't safe. Of course they told us now after my parents had signed all the purchase papers. It was to be our house now. Complete with ghosts and danger. Too late now to look for anywhere else.

Mum made a noise of polite sympathy. The rest of us were silent as we processed this. Roscoe then brought the subject back to the ghost, as if that was a more cheerful topic.

"It's the wife who's said to haunt the place. And there are others... We've heard things haven't we," Roscoe turned to his partner. "The room next to the TV room's the worst."

At this, I could not help myself, I gasped. That was the room I had already chosen to be mine. Now it was making sense, in a bad way. I had come to the house with Dad, just the two of us and Dusty, to muck out the stables while Dad planted trees. He had encouraged me to go, "to get used to the place" and the hard labour involved in owning horses. Roscoe and Coralie had said we could go there in the weekends to do this if we liked and if they weren't there they would leave a key in one of the feed bins. That time, Roscoe wasn't there. I noticed (with surprise) that my father had a long jovial con-versation, laughing with Coralie, while I was doing the hard work, pushing wheelbarrows full of straw across the yard to the compost heap behind the stable yard.

As Dad planted a row of saplings, and my arms wearied of pitchforking and pushing heavy barrow loads, I took a break. I needed to go to the bathroom. I opened the back door, took off my gumboots and left them by the door, I walked through the kitchen, across the hallway and up the flight of deep blue carpeted stairs to the bathroom. I looked at my reflection in the mirror above the sink. Two plaits framed my face. My clear wide-spaced blue-green eyes gazed steadily back. I was wearing a white polo neck jumper and mauve cord trousers. I dried my hands on a towel hanging over the towel rack on the papered wall (displaying a monotone design of semi-naked women), and I surveyed in wonderment the large black sunken bath. As I pushed open the bathroom door it occurred to me to have a look at soon-to-be my room.

As I left the bathroom, I paused and gazed westwards across the hall, at the far end of which was a window-seat beneath a tall sash window. Through the window, I saw a view of the countryside, green fields, and the curve of the mountain on the horizon; the view was reassuring. I took a step onto the flight of stairs to the second floor. As I stepped onto the next stair, I felt a little apprehensive. The house was quiet and still. Despite its modern décor and luxurious fittings, it seemed a little scary. I felt almost as if I was trespassing. But that was ridiculous. It was our house now; I was allowed to be inside. I forced myself to keep on walking up the carpeted staircase. I had set out on my mission with excited anticipation. Modernised and luxurious, The Old Manse with its stable yard far exceeded my wildest dreams of country living. It seemed rather unreal and unbelievable. In truth, the house was too lavish and grand for my taste. It was like a hotel in a James Bond film. As I walked up the staircase I had an uneasy feeling, as if time was slowing down, and I was slowing with it.

I was nearing the landing. On the wall hung two faded sepia portraits. Matching frames held formal photographic portraits of a man and a woman from the nineteenth century. I hadn't noticed them when Roscoe and Coralie had shown my family around the house the first time.

Now I paused, my eyes drawn to the spectral portraits. The gentleman with his handlebar moustache looked authoritative and expressionless, dressed in a dark suit with a high collared shirt; his likeness was faded, indistinct. The woman's image was clearer. She was wearing the corseted dress of a lady. Hair styled in swept-back severity. Her face was pale, attractive, sealed in a distant pensive expression. Neither subject looked as if they'd ever laughed loudly in their lives. I gazed at the images of the couple who had died long ago. They looked as if they were dead when they were photographed; I scared myself with that uncharitable thought. I could see a faint flickering image of my face reflected in the glass of the woman's portrait, luminous and insubstantial, transposed over hers–like a ghost! The thought so scared me, I hurried up the last few stairs to the top floor.

Walking quickly to the room I'd chosen to be my bedroom I placed my hand on the door handle lever and pushed down and out. Nothing happened. I tried it again–the door wouldn't budge. Strange, I thought, there was no visible sign of a lock that I could see, but it must be locked.

Suddenly a wave of cold terror swept over me. It was, I later said, like an icy hand at my throat, pinning me to the spot. I could think of no better way of describing it. (And I had read ghost and horror stories, which I'd found terrifying, it was like something I'd read). It was as if something did not want me to go into that room.

Shaking myself free, I turned and fled. Hand on the wooden banister, I hurried down many flights of stairs. I reached the ground floor, sped along the hallway, grabbed my gumboots, opened the back door and raced outside. After I pulled on my gumboots, I stood in the sunlight, breathing deeply, gulping the air painfully, as if I had been drowning and was now on dry land. "Dusty!" I called. He bounded towards me, hurtling in from somewhere outside the stable yard. I stroked the top of his head and back, and he wagged his tail. His safe, reassuring spirit brought me back to a feeling of normality. I walked around the stable yard until I felt more like myself.

I didn't say anything about this at the time. And I didn't say anything now. After Roscoe and Coralie had finished telling us about the Reverend and his wife, and the tragedy of their children, who'd all died in the house, we had all trooped back downstairs. That was the last time we saw the householders.

As soon as my family moved in, I checked the door of my new bedroom carefully. There was no lock on the inside. Therefore, there was no explanation as to why it hadn't opened, I told Lily, who by now I had related my strange experience to.

I am sure everyone else, like me, wanted to think that the scary stories Roscoe and Coralie had told us were just for entertainment, as they were both actors. But once the stories were in my mind it was impossible not to brood on the idea that our new house really was haunted.

Other things were not entirely explicable. Creaks and noises plagued my nights. Lily and I spent one overcast afternoon shuffling around the living room with our eyes half-closed and arms and hands outstretched. We were convinced that some areas of the airspace in the large room were colder than others. Sometimes Dusty would stand still, growling, as if at a foe, although we could see nothing there. And one night as I lay in bed in my new bedroom, I heard a peculiar dripping sound on the other side of the ceiling, coming from the attic. I called my father who was watching TV and he climbed up into the attic to investigate, the hatch was in the sloped and beamed ceiling of my bedroom, Dad stood on a chair then stepped up onto the sealed fireplace mantelshelf. Dad reported he could see nothing. When he stepped back down into my bedroom, the drip-drip sound started again, juddering all over the ceiling; Lily and Dad and I all heard it.

One night, I woke suddenly and could not return to sleep. *Drip–drip–creak.* I could hear the sounds in the attic above me. My ears strained in the darkness, picking up vibrations.

"Here's to you, Ghost," I said to myself, as I tried to pretend I wasn't scared.

Coralie had told my mother about a horse she knew of for sale, and said it might be ideal for me. It was 14.2 hands high (the measurement of a hand laid sideways, to the withers, the curved bone at the base of the horse's neck, the highest point of the horse's back), so could be called a horse as well as a pony. It was a chestnut gelding with a white blaze down the centre of its face and four white socks.

Dad drove us all to see the horse called Phoenix. I had a ride in a farmland field near a lough. The horse was not very easy to ride, reluctant to canter, skittish, shying at a hawthorn bush as a gust of wind blew up leaves as we trotted by. But I had fallen in love. There was no way I was going to say no, and my parents made the necessary arrangements with the owners. I felt I could hardly speak in case this spell of transformation broke. First our house (slightly spooky though it was), now my horse.

The next day was a Sunday. Phoenix arrived in a horse float pulled by a four wheel drive that drove slowly, the horse float swaying up the driveway, and parked near the front door, in the turning circle. A red-haired man got out of the driver's side, walked to the back of the horse float, opened the doors, pulled down the ramp; went inside, and with some stamping and snorting from the horse, and after a few "Easy"s from the man, the horse was coaxed into stepping backwards, down onto the driveway. A woman in a headscarf and wearing jodhpurs had got out of the four wheel drive, and was talking with my parents, at the front door. Meanwhile I was watching all this avidly. I'd walked out of the house to the parked horse float.

Now I walked up to the horse, and the man handed me the halter rope. The horse still had most of his thick winter coat. I patted his neck; hairs came out in my hand. He'd have his summer coat soon. "Hello Phoenix," I said.

I led Phoenix to the field next to the house, and unclipped the rope, leaving the halter on. I stayed there, looking at him, and talking to him as he walked around, and gave him some hay, to gain his trust. That afternoon I saddled up and rode Phoenix in the front field watched by my family at the gate. I trotted, then cantered, in circles.

After my ride, and removing the tack in the stable yard, I put the halter on Phoenix and led him to the front field where I let him loose, I fetched a bale of hay from the barn, carried it to the field and slipped off the string, spreading out pieces on the ground as Phoenix snorted appreciation. I filled a bucket with water at the yard tap and carried it to the field for my horse. Only then did I pick up the saddle and bridle and my hard hat from where I'd carefully placed them at the back door and carried them inside to the wooden 'horse' (a long structure which Roscoe and Coralie had left behind) in the laundry which doubled as a tack room.

I went for a ride every day, in the afternoons after school, on the weekends, and in the days of the Easter holidays. Dressed in jodhpurs and leather jodhpur boots, string riding gloves, a white shirt, black jacket and black velvet covered riding hat, the clothes I'd worn at riding lessons, horse shows, pony club events, and on treks in England. Soon I would wear jeans, or the loons that I began to wear after I met Margy and became involved in a new way of life here. But that was in the future.

I went riding in the front field, and then after a few days of getting used to Phoenix's paces, I gathered up my courage and headed Phoenix down the driveway, the wind whipping at my hair. Phoenix's chestnut coat and mane shining in the sunlight. I rode along the Lane flanked by hawthorn hedgerows, then turned and rode down another road, and reached a peat bog. Most days would pass with no cars on the road, just an occasional tractor in the fields every few weeks. I trotted along the narrow lane between the expanse of peat bog to one side and, on the other, fields stretching down to the river. I had noticed some girls at school, and our neighbours called peat bogs 'the moss'. They were riddled with pools of dark water, which Ian, the next-door farmer, told us could reach dangerous treacherous depths. He told us that waterlogged peat can act like quicksand, people can fall into it because it's slippery, or tread on it in a bog pool and get stuck, people have died that way he said. It was covered in spongy green sphagnum moss, with heather bushes, and white moss cotton on thin green stems. It was the compression of sphagnum moss in the wetlands that bonded together over hundreds and thousands of years, that turned decaying plants into peat, my father told us.

Dad had rented a section of the peat bog from the farmer who owned the land, after we bought the house. Dad had come home after a shopping excursion with a tool for cutting turf. It resembled a garden spade with two sides, meeting at right angles.

"Who wants to have a go at cutting turf?" he asked. We all did, and so the next day, which was a Sunday, after lunch the family drove to the peat bog to locate our allotted patch. We were the only people in sight. I never saw anyone else there.

Dad parked the van on the verge of short scrubby grass at the side of the flat narrow road that traversed the peat bog. Out here, there was none of the bright green grass that grew high, scattered with wildflowers, on the verges in front of the hawthorn hedgerows that lined the lanes bordering the fields of farmland on the field-side of some of which were ditches filled with water. Here, out on the peat bog, a different sort of vegetation grew over the dark underworld of peat, which was open cut in sections by hand. When it was cut it was called turf.

"Look, a lark!" cried Mum, as I jumped out of the van. A small brown crested bird was rising almost vertically above the bog.

I looked around at the spongy ground, riven by the open gashes of the banks, where turf had long been hand-cut.

Dad was walking carrying the sleán, and Lily and Alex were following in their gumboots. We were all wearing old clothes.

High above, the skylark hovered, singing melodiously.

My mother and Sarah followed the others. I walked behind them.

"Look! A snipe!" called Mum. She was pointing towards a dark pool.

"What's a snipe?" asked Lily loudly.

"It's a wading waterbird; there it is with the long thin pointy beak!" said Mum.

"Stop your sniping!" shouted Alex.

In the black pond, a long-legged, long-beaked brown bird

patterned intricately with gold and brown bars, tilted its head side-to-side, and with a splash and flash of wings flew up from the water, and over to another pool.

"See, you've scared the snipe with all your noise, you've got to be quiet if you want get close to wild birds," I said to my siblings.

"It wasn't us, it was Dusty," said Lily.

As the bird flew off, Dusty, who'd run on ahead, turned. He gave eager chase after it.

"Dusty! Dusty! Come here!" I called.

"Who's shouting now?" said Lily sticking out her tongue at me.

"Well, here it is." My father called. "This is our section."

The family gathered around. Our section was open cut into brown-black peat, the bank was long and deep formed by turf cutters over many years.

"Because it's already been worked, we can just keep cutting it out, otherwise I'd have to slice off the top layer of vegetation to dig into the peat below," Dad said. "It's easier this way."

He picked up the sleán and thrust it into the dark peat. After several tries, he had the angle, he turned the implement and sliced out a cube of the carbon-rich matter.

"Here we are, the first piece of turf. After we've cured it we can burn it in the living room fireplace."

"Is it ill? Hahaha!" shouted Alex.

"That's another word for treating it, or processing it, so that it can burn well, it's too damp now," said Mum, as if it wasn't obvious.

All the Bergsons had a turn at cutting out the peat, only Dad was able to slice out the cube of turf. He explained that the cubes of wet turf needed to be laid out on the ground for a while to dry before they could be burnt as fuel. They had to be turned to let the cubes of turf form a skin before they were "footed" as it was called, four had to be propped up together in a kind of pyramid to let air circulate around them. This helped them to dry and solidify. When they had, they would need to be "rickled" and "clamped." After this process the peat would have dried out into turf to be used as fuel to burn in the home fireplace. He'd been reading about it. Dad would need to be visiting the moss regularly if he wanted to cut and cure enough turf to keep a fire burning at night in the living room fireplace in autumn and winter, I thought.

I set off for a walk with Lily and Alex. Dusty bounding in uneven circles around us.

"You know bodies of murdered people are buried in peat bogs," said Alex.

"Ugh! Do you have to be so gruesome!" shouted Lily.

"I read about it, in a comic," Alex continued.

"A comic. Haha! Very funny!" shouted Lily.

"Don't go near the pool, you might get stuck, like Ian said!" Alex replied at high volume.

I was not giving them much attention. I had seen something extremely odd.

Possibly something alarming.

"Just a minute."

I walked away from my brother and sister, towards what I thought I could see. Were my eyes playing tricks on me?

Little blue flames, flickering in the water of a pool. Lily and Alex joined me.

"I thought I saw a fire!"

I picked up a stick and started poking around stumps of old dead trees at the edge of the brackish water.

"Look!" cried Lily.

Tiny blue flames darted out from a gap the stick imprinted around the black wood.

"What is it?" said Lily, sounding almost frightened.

"It's the fires of Hell!" said Alex.

"It's very strange," I stirred the water.

The flames disappeared but then blue tongues licked out of the old tree again.

"This place is weird," said Lily.

"Let's go and tell Mum and Dad, ask them to come and see."

But when we brought them to the pool there was no sight of the flames.

"We all saw it," I said. "What could it have been?"

Then Dad told us a curious thing.

"It probably was flames. The peat emits vapours which are self-combustible. Once ignited, subterranean peat smoulders and can keep on smouldering. These simmering fires can burn for a very long time, even centuries, slowly moving forwards, burning underground. The flames you saw could have been a fire in layers of peat under the surface, which can sometimes be seen above ground, drawn up through the semi-submerged trees in the pool," Dad explained.

"What did I say? They were flames from hellfire under the ground!" shouted Alex. "And *you* were the one who saw them first!"

He pointed at me.

"Oh, Alex." Mother said. "Daddy has just told us about the fires underground. They're in the peat. That's the explanation."

"It was a joke," said Alex.

"So, there could be a fire burning deep in the ground under

our house and land, from the peat bog? I'm not sure if that is really so reassuring, I think it's quite alarming," I said.

"It's nothing you need to worry about," said Dad. "It's only very occasionally that the flames can appear above ground, as you saw them, you were lucky you did. It's very rare. And, as you saw, they do not stay on the surface long enough to do any damage. And they are found in a damp environment where they can't spread overland. So there's no need to be anxious."

"Interesting," I said.

"Look," cried Mum again, pointing. "A raptor. It's a hen harrier. They live here. It's a male."

We all looked up. The bird of prey was hovering in the air, above us.

"Oh-oh. It's seen something," said Alex.

The bird swooped suddenly to the ground and snatched its prey in its claws.

"Oh, no!" squealed Lily, "it's got something, is it a mouse? Go after it, Dusty!"

Dusty bounded towards it barking, and with a beating of its wings, the powerful bird rose into the air with the creature's neck in its beak and flew out of sight.

"Don't be upset," Dad said to Sarah, who was crying. "It's the nature of the hen harrier. Do you know why they're called hen harriers?"

"No."

"It's because they like to swoop down on hens and eat them. You'll have to keep an eye on our chooks."

That didn't exactly help Sarah, who was nonetheless doing her best to be understanding about it and said that she would look after the chooks, as she dried her eyes.

Back at the house, we all continued the conversation we'd

started earlier about things beneath the surface of the moss.

We were all sitting at the kitchen table, eating home-made soda bread, butter and strawberry jam.

Mum brought in books about peat bogs which we read and found out more about it.

"Listen to this," I said. "Lots of things have been found in peat bogs. Food. Butter! Slabs of butter hundreds of years old have been found, wrapped in cloth, that are still edible!"

"Ugh! That's not true!" said Lily.

"Well, it says here, it is. And bodies have been found in peat bogs."

"So! I was right!" said Alex.

"But the bodies described here are thousands of years old and are believed by archaeologists to have been sacrificed by Druids. The bodies are preserved, mummified in peat bogs, still recognisable as people. Imagine finding an ancient body when you're cutting turf, Dad."

"Well, I think it's very unlikely," Dad replied.

"But how about this. This is what I'd like to find. Jewels and coins have been found in peat bogs too," I said.

"Buried treasure," said Lily.

"Yes, people hide things in the peat bog for various reasons, and then can't find what they've hidden, or they can't get back there."

"Maybe we'll find something really valuable," said Alex.

"You can come with me when I turn the turf," said Dad. "If you help me with the work, you might find something."

Before the Easter holidays I had sat exams, and the results had not been good. Every day that holiday, I went riding on Phoenix.

In the field I set up jumps that I made from fallen branches that I dragged there from behind the house, and I practiced jumping. I was pleased to find that Phoenix liked jumping. I rode along country lanes, in sunshine, and rain. On still blue-skied days and in high winds.

As I trotted along, the rhythmic sound of Phoenix's hooves striking the road was calming.

3

MUM HEARS GHOSTLY VOICES, 1972

Everything seemed to be going well at home. Then Mum told us that something had happened to her that was strange and unsettling. One afternoon she said when the rest of us came home, she had been in the kitchen, when she'd heard children's voices calling "Mummy! Mummy!" from the upper floor of the house.

Mum was so sure she heard this that she told us she called back: "I'm coming!" and she walked into the hallway. Then she remembered we were out with Dad who had taken us with him shopping, and she was on her own. I felt a cold chill. It had never occurred to me that Mum might believe in ghosts and hauntings. That she too might have taken what Roscoe Golightly said seriously. She heard children's voices calling *Mummy! Mummy!* upstairs when we were not in the house! When no one else was in the house! I was scared by her story.

"What do you think it was?" I'd asked, in a small voice.

"I don't know," said Mum.

"It must have been the wind," said Dad briskly. "You only imagined it was voices."

"Yes, that would have been it, Mum," I said brightly.

Soon after that at the start of the summer term, I became ill with a mystery illness. When I tried to get up one morning, my mind and body slipped with vertigo. I could hardly move my limbs. My mother contacted a doctor in the town who made a house call.

Doctor Lyons diagnosed a low-level viral infection and said I must stay in bed until I recovered.

For weeks I was too ill to do anything, I felt detached from everything, I was exhausted, I slept most of the time. As my strength returned, I read a novel that I began in that illness. In the daytime and at night when I was not sleeping, I read. As soon as I started it I was drawn in, as the narrator in their sixties, goes back in memories triggered by an attempt to sort through boxes of things from their past and they find their old diary. The narrator's young self is aged between "twelve and thirteen" at the start as indeed I was, and their birthday was in July, like mine, although a couple of weeks later. I read the book in an immersive trance, the narrative recounted from early adolescence, and it became one of my favourite books.

Weeks later, I announced to Mum: "I think I am well enough to go for a ride!"

"Well, there's no point in going back to school for the last day," Mum agreed, obviously relieved that I was myself again.

"I'll go riding next week. I do still feel tired, but much, much better than I was."

And at the end of the school year in July, my parents were informed by my school principal, Mrs Cavendish-Oxley, that to catch up I must be kept back and repeat second year.

I went riding every day over the summer holidays. Having a brilliant time. I couldn't care less about school, or what the teachers thought of me, I told myself. The subject material was different here. And I didn't care about stories about ghosts, or the strange noises in the house that sounded like children's voices, which was just the wind blowing through the eaves.

The holidays passed too quickly. And now I had to face what I was really dreading. Going back to school.

4
NEW FRIEND, 1972

At first we were diffident, rude, to each other that autumn.

It was impossible for me not to notice that she was a passive attention seeker. She would saunter into the classroom, skirt hitched higher than her knees, tie knot pulled down daringly, an expression of faint contempt on her face. Casually dropping her schoolbag on the desktop beside me, she'd sidle onto the seat as if I wasn't there. Glancing sideways, I registered the signs of her bold independence; the mascara accentuating her long eyelashes. I had not even started to wear make-up and it certainly would have never occurred to me to wear it to school. I looked down resolutely, at the defaced surface of the wooden desk, on which were inscribed anonymous legends: '—is a C***' 'Fuck skool'. Names of local heroes. A few acronyms.

As a diversion I devoted myself to interpreting the scratched initials, trying to figure out what they meant. Over time, I worked out they all stood for Protestant paramilitary groups.

"Hello Margy," I summoned up the courage and said her name and said hello, after weeks of careful silence.

"Hell-o, Roxy," she replied in an exaggerated local brogue, laced with bemusing self-satire. For some reason, Margarita made me think of that bastion of naughty comic schoolgirls, a comedy on TV that I'd watched at one of my friends' houses before we left England, with the sixth form gang of school-girls in short gym tunics, wearing make up and stockings, smoking cigarettes, one was even married, involved in madcap anarchic deeds with junior school girls who wielded hockey sticks. What had indirectly brought about the riotous association was the Preparatory school uniform, which Lily had to wear, which Mum had laughed about before we moved here (and which of course I did not wear as I was in the grammar school).

In the Prep school, the uniform included gym tunics and girdles for girls. Girdles? I'd questioned my mother as she read out from the prospectus before we came here, when we were still living in the village of Little Hampton, in Somerset.

"It's a kind of belt, a long piece of fabric worn around the waist that is tied at the side," Mum had explained. It had been a few months before our move, we were sitting around the kitchen table, Mum (to my surprise) laughing incredulously at the requirements and the regulations outlined in the school rule book. "Girdles and gym tunics! And in Senior School a prefects' lawn. Prefects! It's like going back in time!" As I was going to have to attend the school I didn't really consider it amusing. I had found the prospect of it all quite daunting, but I hid my trepidation and laughed along with the others.

"Hockey!"

"I played hockey at school," admitted Mum. "It's not a bad game."

"Jolly hockey sticks!" I cracked up in a fit of forced hysterics as if nothing could be funnier.

Lily had to wear a gym tunic, girded by a girdle. But as I was in the grammar school, I wore a grey skirt, white shirt, black cardigan, and grey and black tie. (After I met Margy, I too would undo my top shirt button, pull the knot of the tie lower, and roll up the waistband of my skirt).

It all seemed "unbelievably antiquated" to my mother (who had worn similar garb at her private girls' school in Sydney, a million years earlier, no doubt minus the modifications). Yet as it turned out, Lily did not go into the grammar school after Prep. My brother who was doing well nonetheless had to leave too with her so she would not have to travel alone by bus to their new school in another town. They even caught another bus from the other end of the lane. So I did not spend as much time with them both as I would have otherwise done if we'd all stayed at the same school. I was on my own a lot, travelling to and from school by bus, and at school.

I first met Margy at the start of the autumn term, after I turned thirteen. It was a shock to me that my grades were so bad I must repeat the year. Having come from a very different school system in England I was hardly prepared in subjects I'd never studied before. Algebra, Latin, Geometry, Chemistry… My mind froze in disbelief at my grades in my first exams. My English and Art grades were as high as they'd been in England, the rest a surreal joke. 9% for Chemistry. 2% for Maths! And that was before I fell ill with the long mystery illness.

But, as time went by, I managed to almost convince myself that I felt more pride in these startling new marks than I had for my grades at my previous school in England (where I was learning binary arithmetic). I had been in the A stream for all graded subjects without trying particularly hard. I'd been plunged into a world of the logically absurd and, as in a surreal dream, grown bigger and more uncomfortably visible in my academic dungeon. This mortifying plunge from grace was hastened by the open derision of some of my new teachers. Which was why I was compelled into what I saw to be the only sane option. Inner defiance. It had begun in the first term I was there. Margy, on the other hand, had moved from her previous class into 2B on her parents' wishes, because, she confided, they thought she was not getting along well with the other girls. Maybe there were more complicated reasons behind it. But whatever they were, at the beginning of second year in September 1972 we were two new girls in a mixed-sex class of closed pairs. At first we sat together only because there weren't enough old wood and iron desk-and-chair sets for us to each sit alone and maintain the state of isolation we both claimed to prefer.

Margy and I did not look dissimilar. Later, when we hung out together, people asked if we were sisters. We were both tall and slim, with long straight hair and pale complexions. I was a little taller. Her eyes were the colour of blue light. Mine were an indecisive blue green. Her hair was black. Mine, reddish-brown.

Before long I, rather diffidently, asked Margy if she would like to come home with me after school one afternoon. And, after a hesitant pause, Margy said yes, she would ask her mum, her tone of voice was suddenly warm and friendly.

5
OUT-OF-SCHOOL WITH MARGY, 1972

Margy said she liked our house. Her own family home, I was to find, was larger and older. She said they did not have central heating, and that winter was cold. By early December, the ground was covered in frost well into the morning, and it was dark just after five pm.

We got out at the top of the lane and walked the half a mile to the stone gateposts and wrought iron gates, then up the drive. The chill was such that we could see clouds of our exhaled breath vaporising as we talked and walked. I showed her around. The stabled ponies, the cats, the chickens in the stable with a few bricks removed from the back wall so they could walk outside and range around freely in the small field. I introduced her to Dusty, and my family, those who were home and who were not unsociably in their rooms. By the end of the two hours Lily and Sarah, and my brother had all put in a brief appearance and said hello, as Margy and I made cheese on toast and instant coffee in the kitchen, and of course, Mum was there. Welcoming, talking in her warm way, making Margy feel at home. Each carrying our coffee and snack, I'd taken Margy up to my room, which she said she liked. The record player was in my room then and I played her my singles.

"I think they've all been released on their albums except the latest. Y'know it was released last August; it could be on their next album." Margy considered this and said her favourite band at the moment was another one, that I thought was okay too.

Margy's father, Humphrey, arrived in his car to collect her at six pm. He and mum started chatting in the downstairs hall near the front door and they did not move away from that spot and say goodbye for what seemed like ages. It turned out they had lots to talk about. They both liked to talk. Their conversation sounded like Mum talking with her friends back in England. They got on. We all got on. That was an exhilarating feeling.

Margy's house was several miles from our house, situated in the fields of another glen. I arranged with Margy to meet the next Saturday when we went on shopping trips to Ballyhope with our fathers. All the town centres were fenced with barricades manned by soldiers, to try to prevent car bombs. We parked opposite a church and walked from there. My dad shopped for the groceries. Margy's father was going to check if parts for his tractor had arrived, she'd said. Margy and I were allowed to spend an hour on our own together. Chaperoned by our dads we met in the burger cafe, one of a franchise chain with white, orange and brown decor and liberal use of plastic. It served milkshakes and juices. Our dads departed to do their shopping.

By coincidence, Margy and I arrived clad in variations of the local high street store Shezam's purple suede jacket with a cream fake fur collar. I wore a shorter style; Margy's was longer and waisted. Each had a zipper up the front. Both of us were wearing flared cords, polo neck jumpers and platform shoes, in different shades and styles.

Neither of us had known what the other would be wearing, and yet we had dressed almost identically.

When I walked in and saw Margy waiting, sitting at a table by the window, we'd looked at each other in feigned fury, she burst out laughing, so did I, we were both pleased.

"You got your jacket at Shezam?"

"Yeah, I was going to get the one you have."

"It looks good."

"So does yours."

"Did you get your platforms at Merley's?"

"Yeah, I saw yours there, and I almost got them, but then I got green and brown."

"They look great."

"So do yours."

"Do you want a soft drink?" asked Margy.

"I think I'll have a natural orange juice."

Margy had the same.

We sipped our drinks as we sat opposite each other; Margy facing the back wall over my shoulder, me looking out at the street. Talking, and not looking at each other for more than a second. I realised she was definitely cool.

The following Saturday afternoon we met in town again, driven by our respective fathers who were doing supermarket shopping, we were allowed to spend an hour shopping for books with our pocket money. I was wearing a blue and cream stripy polo neck with mauve cords with bell bottoms. Margy wore a rust, caramel and cream stripy jumper, and jeans with bell bottoms. We each wore our purple jackets, and platform shoes.

We stood staring at each other in dramatized disbelief for a moment, and burst out laughing together at the same time, even more secretly pleased at our shared taste.

That first weekend, I saw that Margy wore blue eye shadow, mascara accentuating her long eyelashes, and brown lipstick. The next weekend, I wore brown eye shadow and brown lip gloss that I had bought in town. It was the era of makeup and fashion; we both watched the weekly music chart topping show and I sometimes read a teenage girl magazine, which had advertisements and advice on how to get the latest looks; we might not have been able to get those cosmetics here but there were similar shades. We each wore our hair loose with a centre parting, secured with hair grips. By the time we discovered we both liked the same books and music, films, and telly shows, liked the same girls and found the same boys fanciable, we had become what many would describe as 'best friends'. But 'best friends' was not how we termed ourselves. 'Best friend' sounded conventional and we saw ourselves as being different. Also, though I did not dwell on it, it reminded me of my 'old' best friends I'd left in England and everything here in my new life had to be different. (Or it would feel like a kind of betrayal). I later referred to us as 'close friends'. In what seemed like no time, my new friend was coming home with me after school and staying the night.

6

NEW BEGINNINGS, 1973

It was early in the spring term. Mum had, wonderfully, got her licence and Sarah had started Kindergarten, in the Prep school. Grandmother in Sydney had bought Mum a car as a gift for taking driving lessons. Every school day Mum drove Sarah and I to school, and she collected Sarah each afternoon after school. The infants' years came out earlier than senior school, but Mum said if I liked she would wait and drive me home too. *If I would like.* I had not told her about the school bus gauntlet. Same as I had not told my parents about the after-school detentions I'd been put in starting last year and having to hitch hike back as the last bus had left by the time I was let out of the detention room. I'd had to walk through the town, through the army barricades, once past a gang on the other side of the road who threw stones and called out things at me ("Is she English?"), *Piss Off, just piss off,* I had shouted silently, as I hurried past to the single lane country road out of town, as darkness fell, and then stuck out my thumb when I heard a car behind me, as I had no other way of getting home. It was too far to walk at that time. Thankfully I was given lifts each time by men who did not question me, nor seem to want to talk either, and who stopped their cars when I asked, and let me out. I was lucky. I walked down the lane and up the drive to our house, arriving back well after six pm. My father was not yet home and Mum was busy with all the things she had to do, and she never asked me why I was so late and what had I been doing. It did not occur to me to tell her I'd been in detention and had to hitch home. It was too annoying to have been put into detentions, which was happening every school day it seemed, before I became friends with Margy. Mainly my detentions were for forgetting. School books, my home-work, my exercise book. All very annoying. When I started to sit beside Margy she would share her schoolbooks with me, if I forgot mine, she seemed sympathetic and smiled at me. She did not turn on me. I was relieved and grateful. That was how we had started to be friends.

But now, miraculously, it seemed all the bad stuff was over. I would not need to catch the school bus again now that Mum came to collect Sarah, and me. I would never need to run all the risks it carried. And I was no longer being put into after school detention. In Mum's car as we drove along the country roads to and from school, I felt immune to all the threatening elements outside.

Then Margy stayed the weekend, for the first time. Then she stayed again. "This is my fourth daughter!" Mum would introduce my friend at my parents' parties for Dad's colleagues, at The Old Manse. Hand-cut turf smouldered in the fireplace that winter, and spring. Mum did the catering. The pinnacle was her cheesecake, which one of Dad's work colleagues from New York fed me a forkful of from her serving, as I stood with her in the crowded living room, I'd asked her if it was savoury. It was not; it was sweet, creamy, and delicious.

Margy of course stayed in my room. We slept in my bed. Lily and Alex occupied bedrooms on the opposite side of the carpeted hallway. Little sister Sarah slept in her own bedroom on the first floor opposite my parents' bedroom.

Now when I came home from school, I felt good about life. After I had fed and watered the ponies, and other animals, and made a snack of cheese on toast in the kitchen, I ran up the flights of stairs to my bedroom. I lay on my bed, reading. I had stopped worrying about every stressful detail of my day: a habit which had plagued me since we left England. Through the window floated the sounds of birdsong and the lowing of cows; I could smell the hawthorn hedge below the window. Swallows flitted to and fro under the eaves, building nests. My latest reading was a paperback book of new Japanese writing that Dad had brought back from a work trip to Japan and given to me.

As I read the words from another culture on the other side of the world, I slipped into an intense, pleasurable, dream-like state, that of the profoundly anguished, and exquisite realm of pure, mad poetry. (I told myself that and tried to believe it). Although the story about the narrator disembowelling himself, which the author had recently done, committing ritual suicide and eviscerating himself before the book was published, lent a confusing horror to reading enjoyment. It seemed the stories and poems were edged with trauma. The post-World War Two writings were significant.

I also loved to lie on my bed and listen to the sitar album

that Dad had brought back from a work trip, tantalising my senses like a promise from the future calling out to me. On those brilliant, shining, blue-skied spring afternoons I felt in love with life, the infinite possibility beckoning me with sweet intensity. I could feel the wild, reckless power of growing.

Even more, I loved to sit or lie on my bed with Margy next to me, as we rambled in serious and laughing turns, about so many things. Boys we fancied; girls in our class who we agreed seemed so much younger than us, and in fact were. We were a few months older than the cohort, both of us, we'd discovered, having had bouts of ill health compelling us to repeat a year.

The question that hovered over us was what did we want to do when we left school, what would we do when we grew up, and left home? To go to university, or art school, required doing well in exams, getting good O Levels and then A Levels. Staying on at school to do that. That was where I hoped I was heading although I did not dare say it. I had notched up such a dubious start at my new school that I might as well be going to school on Mars, compared to how well I had done at school in England.

I preferred to think about other questions that were not so stressful.

What does it mean to be a human?

What is the purpose of life?

Well, what is it?

We were not sure.

"I used to say I preferred animals to humans," I confided to Margy. "Dad would ask me as we sat at the Sunday dinner table: 'If there was a burning house and there were upper floor windows, one with a person in it, and the other with a dog, and you could save one only, which one would you save?'"

"What did you say?"

"I didn't really know what to say. I think he was trying to challenge me. To think about the ethical question. I knew if I said 'the dog' what the reaction would be. I was being pushed into a corner."

What is reality; what is illusion? Reality is illusion conjured from our sensory perception. Margy concurred with me.

What happens to you when you die?

It's impossible to imagine it when you're alive, we agreed.

What if there is a nuclear war... if a nuclear bomb dropped here, like Hiroshima or Nagasaki? The thought of what had happened there terrified us. Gazing through my window at the starry sky and moonlit fields, which looked etched forever in time, out of time. We talked and talked. Our heads next to each other, on a shared pillow.

The months passed and Margy and I became closer friends. When she came to visit, we rode the ponies, me on Phoenix, she on Crackers, Sarah's pony; I arranged jumping courses in the front field. We took it in turns to jump. But then, one day, Margy confessed that really she was frightened of horses and opted to stay inside with Lily. Margy was becoming friends with Lily too. After that, when I knew Margy was coming to visit, I put the ponies in the front field so they did not need to be exercised after school. (I still went riding of course and I taught Sarah to ride).

Sometimes Margy and I went for walks behind the house to the river.

We were tending to do the things that Margy liked to do.

We invented new ages for ourselves.

"We're eighteen!" we chorused, at age fourteen, the first

time we went to Sliders, a popular hotel disco bar in Portrush. Margy's older brother, Sheridan, who had just got his license, drove us there and back, and acted as our chaperone. Neither set of parents seemed worried about our excursion, as unfazed as Margy and I were by the possibility of bombs in the venues –which happened on occasion, but never when we were there. It was one of those things that you just hoped would never happen. Despite the conflict (war) waged across the province, we lived our lives as normally as possible.

7

ROAD TRIP TO PORTUGAL 1973

Margy and I were both delighted when her parents accepted my parents invitation for her to come on our road trip holiday to Portugal, which was Dad's way of taking us with him on his work trip to Lisbon, renting a villa in Costa da Caparica, the holiday resort on the coast for a month, sandwiched between driving overland from Northern Ireland, crossing via car ferry to France, over the Pyrenees into Spain, across the dusty plains to Portugal, staying at campsites on the way there, and back. (I can see now that he did not want to leave us without him for any length of time at The Old Manse).

I kept a journal I made from a bunch of folded A4 copy paper, that I titled My Trip. When I had to move recently I found this in a box with many other old writings and objects from earlier times, which have triggered these memories, of a time in my life that I later forgot for decades.

Wow. If yesterday was uneventful to-day completely made up for it. Read on and find out what happened on this day–an ordinary Thursday for some but not for us. It started out nicely. Margy, Lily and I slept in and I was woken up by Alex who gave me a lovely ring–a ring with a lozenge and the letter R on it–a belated birthday present. The others prompt-ly gave him some money and he went out and bought an 'M' ring and an 'L' ring–We got up and had breakfast. Dad was going to Lisbon and we said good-bye to him because he was going early. We had lunch and decided to go down to the beach. We put on our bikinis and set out. We went down and found it was the yellow flag again. The waves were huge but we splashed gaily into the water when to our horror we found out we were being followed by two yucky dudes. Well we put our little brains together and came to this brilliant conclusion
– We would move on. We moved along the beach and they followed us. Oh deary-me! One escape route–the sea. We splashed merrily into the briny. They waved to us and we gave them the finger (how sociable). We came out and began to sunbathe completely ignoring them and then three cheers they walked away. We cheered and clapped and they gave us filthy looks. Lily and I went into the sea and saw what we thought was just two men but really they had another man with them. An anxious crowd had gathered on the beach. They dragged the man in and the crowd pressed round him. He was putty-coloured and his lips were purple. He was drowned. They tried to bring him back to life by pumping the water out of his lungs and mouth to mouth resuscitation.

He was covered up and taken away. I felt very faint–it was the first time I had seen a dead person. After this a crowd of fellas went into the sea–really deep and in the same place as the man had been. We told them how stupid we thought they were and stayed talking for a few mins. Then we decided to go home. On the way we talked to two fellas with fuzzy hair (lovely looking) who were Portuguese. When we got home we had tea. After tea, Margy, Lily and I went out for a little walk. We came back and went to bed and talked for ages.

To J

Every day the sun burnt a hole
In the eggshell blue sky
It crept into our hair and bodies
And filled us with happiness
And light.
We saw each other constantly
And everything was beautiful
Because I was on holiday.
People staring in the streets
But we laughed.
Together.
We splashed in the sea
And watched the sun set.
In a mist of golden memories
Everything was a beautiful dream
And then I woke up.

(Oct 73)

8

BOYS, 1973

After the summer holidays, Margy and I fell for boys at school. Fellas was the term in magazines for teenage girls that mum had subscribed to in England for me. We danced with boys/ fellas who asked us in the dark gym at the school disco at night. The protocol I found out was the boy might then ask you to sit down, either you said yes or no. If yes, you sat on the wooden chairs against one of the walls. I danced with Brynn, a Lower-Sixth former, to hits spun by an Upper Sixth form DJ. Then I sat down with him, secretly filled with trepidation.

A few paired bodies along the shadowy rows of partners, sat Margy with Brynn's twin. I was glad when all this was over. It seemed the right thing that we were both pleased we had been asked to dance and sit down. They were nice, polite boys who Margy and I had talked to in the lunchroom, after we'd eaten our sandwiches, during the last few weeks. (We would smile awkwardly in the school corridors when we passed each other for ever after). Then we were driven home by Sherry, Margy's brother (who was in Fifth Form), he dropped us off at my house at just after eleven pm. It made me uncomfortable but I followed Margy's lead.

Margy and I laughed ourselves to sleep, in my bed.

"Let's lie like spoons," was Margy's frequent request. (There was so little space).

"Okay," I rolled over, not giving her enough room. "Shove over would ye, yer great lump!" she commanded in her local brogue, as I mock-fell off the bed, both of us in fits of hysterics before we fell asleep.

50

9

THE GANG OF SEVEN, 1973-4

We hung out with a group of friends, the Gang of Seven or The Seven, Lily called us (this was after she and Alex had changed school). Lily's friend, Bee, whose father worked at the university, had just recently arrived from England too. Dora and Carly, two sisters more or less my age, had moved here, to the school, from London. Same with Tessa. Along with Lily, we were all similar ages, born within three years of each other. With the exception of Margy, we were a band of newcomers and outsiders; we visited and stayed overnight at each other's houses, we wore jeans with bell bottoms, wide legged flared loons, and cords (corduroy trousers), tank tops, tee shirts, midi skirts, platform shoes. We watched Top of the Pops, listened to the same music. We burnt incense, joss sticks, read books, liked poetry, art, music. Cheesecloth smocks and denim. Love beads. We all hoped to go to university or art school after we finished school.

The Seven made ourselves sick gorging on Roman feasts. We got tipsy for the first time together. One overcast afternoon, Lily, Dora, Bee, Margy and I climbed the shelves to the top of the walk-in pantry in the kitchen at my house. There was an open storage space at the top of the shelves, connecting the two wall cupboards of the pantry. Dad kept a reserve supply of spirits there. As we girls made our ascent of the pantry shelves, we bantered.

"For the exercise, girls–jolly hockey sticks now!"

"Hurry on there!"

"*Be careful, ye gurn[1] ye!*" hissed Margy to Lily.

---

1   **Gurn** verb to moan (Scots-Irish dialect)

Mum entered the kitchen.

"Shush…!" I whispered as we hid, choking on laughter, perched, sipping spirits in spluttering turns from the bottle.

"You know koalas get out of it on gum leaves, they get so stoned they fall off their perches!" I hissed at Margy, who was crushed precariously against me. Mum was pottering about, methodically slicing cow hearts on the chopping board. She had exchanged free range eggs from our hens for a sack of offal from Mr Heggarty the butcher in town. Our hens laid many eggs daily. Now, in the tack room next to the kitchen there was always a sack of dead animal innards for Mum to cut up for Dusty. Her intention was commendable. "It's so much better for his coat than tinned meat!" she said. But the smell of offal was disgusting to my vegetarian olfactory perception.

I could make out Mum's shape through the louvre slats of the cupboard door. "There you go, Dusty, good dog…there's a nice bloody chamber for yer," I whispered.

We smothered our giggles as Mum opened the pantry doors and walked in to find an ingredient, never guessing we were all up there drunk as koala bears, not far above her head. Mum was listening to the news on her transistor radio. "Fourteen civilians were killed, ten wounded when a bomb exploded in the Falls Road, in Belfast, this morning." "Two adults and five children were killed and six adults wounded when a petrol bomb exploded in the Bogside in Derry at lunchtime today."

Mum listened to the terrible news all day long and in the evening. She kept her transistor with her. It seemed hard to believe but she did not seem to have noticed we were huddled on the pantry self, as she didn't look up. In England, she had listened to a long-running serialised radio drama, a quiz show, and social comment. She would sometimes laugh then. She did not laugh when she listened to the news of petrol bombs, car bombs, sniper attacks, shootings, murders, many of the victims of murders, killings and hideous injuries were children and innocent civilians.

My friends Dora and Carly held parties and we danced and lay on the floor. My bedroom walls were hung with posters I'd bought in a record shop in Coleraine; and one of a photograph of the horses of the Camargue cantering through surf. Margy's eldest brother who'd moved to Canada had assembled a record collection which he'd left in his room in their house. Margy played the albums when I visited and I discovered the sixties sounds of progressive rock.

The Seven stayed at Dora and Carly's country house when their parents were there; we stayed one night when their parents were in London and, just having fun, we held a strange witchy ceremony in the long drive leading to the road, at midnight in the moonlight, scaring ourselves with the power of the bright silver light, the mound and circle of a hawthorn hedge; the faerie fort in a hill field grew darker, larger, as we improvised vocal chants, and then turned as one and scarpered back to their house. We held seances in the living room of The Old Manse with a homemade ouija board. The glass moved to the letters to spell words. "You're pushing it!" "I'm not!" Of course I hoped that one of us was pushing the glass if it moved. None of us really wanted there to be a ghost, or spirit beings in the house. Then one or more did begin to push it deliberately and spell out comical words to 'break the spell' and the fear that we felt. I had played similar games at my last school. There had been a rumour that was becoming hysterical that the girls changing room in the gym was haunted. I'd taken part one lunchtime in a test by a group of girls, someone turned off the light. We'd sat in a row staring at a wall which we could not see as it was dark, to observe if a ghostly form would manifest. One girl, then another, said they could see something and the light was turned on. It was rumoured the Physical Education teacher was arranging for a psychical researcher to visit the school to do tests on the Girls Changing Room and give their verdict. My family had moved before that happened. We also played another game that I learned one lunchtime.

Levitation.

I lay on the floor, my eyes closed. There was a girl kneeling at my head, one at my feet and one at each side of me. "Take your two index fingers and place them under the girl, fingers relaxed but pointing up," the leader at my head said.

Then it began.

"There's been an accident," the leader intoned.

"*There's been an accident,*" the others repeated.

"A girl's hurt."

"*A girl's hurt.*"

"Badly hurt."

"*Badly hurt.*" I felt myself fall backwards into darkness, as if falling down a well.

"I think she's dying."

"*I think she's dying.*"

"She is dying."

"*She is dying.*"

"I think she's dead."

"*I think she's dead.*"

"She is dead."

"*She is dead.*" I felt utterly inert.

"GAS!" They all intoned loudly together.

At that point the "body" is supposed to levitate.

"Ahh! She's moving, I felt her lifting up!" shouted Bee.

I sat up.

"Phew." We made noises of relief. We laughed and pushed down any real fear any of us might have felt. We only played this a couple of times as we scared ourselves in the supposedly haunted living room with its inexplicable changes in temperature. The first time I was the leader and taught the others. The next time, Dora was the leader. The strange thing was, when it had been me who was the victim, I really felt as if I was slightly lifting up.

10
THE STRIKE, 1974

In May 1974 there was the general strike. There was some notice given via radio and television before it began. My parents stocked up with supplies, shopping at the supermarket in the local town so that we were prepared and able to eat enough. In the two-week strike, power stations were shut down, the electricity grids turned off, roads were blocked, and food was not delivered to the shops not even essentials of milk and bread. (This did not too badly affect Margy's family, who had a dairy herd; and baked soda bread as did we). We had oil lamps, the flimsy metal ones with a wick from a camping store that we used when we went camping. And antique oil lanterns with etched glass shades that Mum had bought in a shop in Ballycastle, and we had these ready when the power was turned off.

For a week-and-a-half every evening we struck matches, lit the lamps, and carried them everywhere we went, one each, up and down the stairs, to our rooms, as sharp swaying shadows surrounded us. As if we'd gone back in time to over a hundred years ago. To the time when the house was a manse and the minister and his wife and their children all still lived here.

There was no petrol, and no public transport.

Dad had bought bicycles for himself, me, Lily and Alex. My brother and I cycled to school in different directions. Dad cycled to work at the university, leaving with Alex. (Lily and Sarah stayed at home with Mum). I set off alone peddling on my bike to school.

Margy rode her bike to school too. We arranged to meet on our bikes at the top of the lane. She cycled several miles to get there. It was about six miles from my house. I brought her a chocolate truffle; one each. Before we set off to cycle along the Ridge Road we popped them into our mouths.

"Mmm!" "Delicious!"

We pedalled off together through the sparkling morning. I followed my close friend. Even the air seemed to be shining. I felt transcendent with joy. The best things about riding a bike were the independence and freedom. Even better if you were with a close friend.

11

I SAVE LILY'S LIFE, 1974

Laughter was the main way our friendship expressed itself and bond deepened. As our shared jokes, put-on voices and joshing developed into a kind of private language we would laugh uncontrollably for what seemed like forever. We laughed and laughed. I couldn't count how many times I was thrown out of class for laughing (never Margy only me, I was the only one of us who was punished, most unfairly really).

But laughter could be physically dangerous. One evening when Lily and I were both at Margy's house, alone with her in the kitchen after tea, we had finished the washing up and were eating biscuits made that day by Margy's mum, and talking and laughing, hysterically. As Lily took a bite of biscuit, Margy said something which set us off again, roaring with laughter.

Lily inhaled and the next moment was gasping for air, she could not breathe, the biscuit had gone down the wrong way and now her face was turning purple. I patted her on the back, but it made no difference. Sherry rushed into the room and patted her on the back too. That did not help either. She was gasping, and before our eyes–dying. I had gone to First Aid classes in England, and I knew what to do. I hit her with the side of my hand between her shoulder blades.

"You'll hurt her, stop!" said Margy.

"Not so hard!" said Sherry.

"I have to do this," I said, in a terrible panic, determined not to lose my sister.

I hit her again and the biscuit dislodged.

12

PERSEPHONE, 1974
Versailles, France

Because of what happened on our holiday last summer in Portugal when she came with us, Margy was not allowed by my parents to come on our road trip holiday to France with us. I sent my close friend missives with self-decorated envelopes from the apartment where myself, my siblings and Mum were staying, in a small town, which belonged to one of Dad's colleagues, who was away somewhere working, like Dad. I pined for my friend. I walked and found a post box where I posted the missives daily; the rest of the time I wrote, read and played board games with the kids. Lily and I walked to Versailles one hot day, to the palace of Louis the Fourteenth. The Sun King. We walked around a massive, geometrically designed formal garden. But it was not the same without Margy.

Autumn Term 1974

English and Art were the two school subjects I most enjoyed. The teachers were not unkind to me. I was relieved and grateful for that–although I could hardly believe it would last. I wasn't laughed at; my love of poetry and reading were not belittled. My writings were published in the school magazine and I had even been awarded a school poetry prize for one of my poems, much to my astonishment.

My English class was working on 'Mythology'.

"For your term project you will choose a mythological story, from any culture. In your assessment work you will approach the mythological narrative from different angles, re-telling the myth." The English teacher, Miss Beckett, was writing on the board as she was speaking.

"First you will contextualise and summarise the myth you have chosen, re-telling its story in your own words. For your next assessment, you will write a poem based on your myth. For the third assessment, you will use the myth as a metaphor in another poem or a story you will write yourselves. You can explore the use of metaphor in all the pieces you write, or in the third piece specifically."

That should be interesting, I thought, glancing around the class at my peers. (My eyes bouncing away from the boys from the school bus and their talk of tractors and combine harvesters).

In Classics, it had to be said, being traditional was a distinct advantage. And in this area the grammar school excelled. Latin was an optional subject, and the classics were woven into the humanities and arts subjects on the curriculum.

I had read versions of classical mythology, in books, since I was much younger. The class was told to decide upon their myth and bring it into class to discuss. Taking it in turns, each student had to enlighten the class about their choices.

"Margarita?"

"I'm working on the myth of Leda and the Swan."

"Roxanne?" Miss Beckett looked at me.

"I'm looking at the Abduction of Persephone."

There were sniggers from some boys in the class.

"Can you tell the class something about this myth?"

"It's a classical Greek mythological story about the young goddess, Persephone, who is both the goddess of new life and rebirth and the Queen of the Underworld or Hades. The myth is believed to have originated as a form of worship, and a symbolic explanation for winter and the seasons, and why it is that seeds planted underground germinate and grow upwards towards the sun in spring and summer. But it also has other resonances to do with rebirth and renewal, and death."

Miss Beckett smiled kindly at me.

"Alright, thank you. Violet?"

Two months later, I delivered my presentation to the class.

"So," I said. "That is the point. It's paradoxical but symbolic. New life comes from underground, from the earth."

"Would you read out your poem to the class?" the teacher asked.

Feeling self conscious, I opened my book and read it out.

Persephone's Abduction

Whirling darkness
Asleep in my bed
The sky of my dreams is gold and blue
Radiant with ancient light
I am playing with my girlfriends by a peaceful pool
Beneath a canopy of trees
Picking spring flowers, piling baskets high
Lilies and violets and carefree daisies
I fill my skirts with fresh perfumed blossoms
I have more than any of them.

From far off, warning sounds
Galloping hoof-beats, sudden darkness
Above us, birds shriek, take flight

He bursts into my golden dream-world
Hades, ruler of the Underworld
Fierce and mighty
Towering in his chariot
Above four plunging horses
He fixes me with a stare
Of fire and thunder
Hypnotized, I cannot move
He lunges at me, grabs me with his mighty hand
I scream
I see my girlfriends' faces freeze in shock
Struggling, I rip my dress, trying to escape

My flowers scatter to the winds
His massive arm clasps me to him
GO! He roars to each steed in turn
The horses rear into a gallop
I scream again
And I
Am gone

(2004)

In the exams I came first in English, second in Art (Margy came first), and in the top five for all the subjects except maths and chemistry although I passed. Margy was in the top five for all subjects, without trying too hard. That motivated me; I hid my relief at getting better marks again.

13
"CATHOLIC OR PROTESTANT?" 1974

"What are ye?" The boy's pale face twisted into a challenging snarl.

"What do you mean?" I pushed my hands into the pockets of my jeans and stared at him. He'd stepped out from behind a car as Margy and I were walking down the Esplanade towards the funfair at Portrush.

"D'yer mean are we–Lesbians?" Margy said putting on an exaggerated local voice.

"No!" he sounded deeply shocked, "I mean are ye Catholic or Protestant?"

This was the leading, loaded question asked on the streets

that was supposed to define and decide things. One of my good friends was Catholic. In sectarian areas there were local people who were the best of friends despite their religion, or lack thereof, I'd heard a young wit hilariously explain this paradox away along the satirical lines of: "I hate all Catholics except Jummy of course, but that's because he's my best mate. And Donal's a Mick but he's a great man." Or: "I hate Protestants except my friend Maureen, but that's because she's my friend since we were waens.[2]" Everyone crowded around him listening to his stories, one afternoon at a party Bee held at her house, we cracked up in hysterics. It was all great craic. All the 'funnier', more tragically ironic, for being true. Like the story told to me by a fella who lived in Belfast. He said he had two badges on his denim jacket. A Catholic badge and a Protestant one. When he was walking in a Catholic area he buttoned up his lapel to show the Catholic badge; when he was walking in a Protestant area he turned his lapel down to reveal the Protestant badge on the other side. To stay safe.

"I'm neither," I replied nonchalantly. "I'm Australian."

"Australian, are ye?" He was taken aback. "Ye don't sound Australian."

"Yeah, well," my tone was deliberately long-suffering, "My parents are Australian, and they like to travel."

"Well," he continued. "Don't they have religion out there?"

"Not like here," I said blithely. "In Australia they don't kill each other in the name of God. At least not that I'm aware of. At least not any more. At least I hope not."

To my surprise, the boy laughed. "Ye're a cheeky one, aren't ye?" he said, keeping pace with us. "Where are ye girls goin' now? To the amusement arcades? I'm goin' that way mesel'…"

---

2   **Waen** (pronounced wee-un or wane) baby or child.

Although it may have sounded like a defensive smart arse answer designed to deflect (like much of my communication with the Outside World then), I was telling what I believed to be the truth. My mother and father were Australian. They had left Sydney a long time ago. I was born in London and grew up in England. I looked English and sounded English. To make the issue of identity more complicated Dad's family was Scottish and English, descended from the Vikings. Mum had been adopted. Although Mum would not talk about it. (It was my Sydney grandmother-by-adoption who'd told me). I wondered if Mum's birth family might have been Irish. My family ancestry on my mother's side could be Irish. What gave me the feeling that my mother's lost family heritage was Irish? Did she say that at some time and I had forgotten? Lily also had an idea that Mum's family was from Ireland. And she did not know how she had that idea, either. (Margy guessed that Mum was descended from nobility, which was interesting to contemplate but only between the three of us).

Maybe that was why I felt confused so much of the time. I didn't know who I really was. I also didn't know how I was supposed to behave. Was I supposed to act aggressively and defend myself?

Or was I supposed to let myself be bullied, and victimised, torn apart with insults, humiliating put downs, and threats of violence. I couldn't do that. I didn't care what 'they' thought I was 'supposed' to do or not do—whoever they were in the gangs, on the streets, and on the buses. But when I stuck up for myself, I got into more trouble.

Here, wherever you went on the streets or on public transport there could be gangs of kids asking what you were staring at;

throwing stones, threatening to kick heads in, or a gang of boys chasing you and your friends, threatening to rape you. That had happened to me, Margy, Lily, Bee, and Dora when we went on an outing one day to a seaside town on the train by ourselves. As we walked around an empty concreted paddling pool by the edge of the beach, a gang came running down the steps from the street and surrounded us. Said they were from Belfast and were in an illegal paramilitary organisation. We girls ran to the street, and rushed into a small supermarket, a couple of the gang followed us in and were chasing around the aisles. We were pleading with the shopkeeper to get help; but he ordered us out of the shop. Terrified, we girls stayed in the shop as long as we could, until after the boys had left and when we left we saw them running away, we shouted at them the police were coming. In the towns, and villages and fields, there could be danger anywhere. There had even been a bomb scare on the bridge crossing the river, not far from The Old Manse. I knew I had to be ready to defend myself at any moment. I was becoming increasingly stressed and paranoid.

"The school system here is thirty years behind England," I overheard Mum say to her friends in England on the phone. And maybe that explained it, maybe that's all it was, a simple soothing explanation. Local life was just stuck in a time warp, caught in the 'wrong' time and space zone, and that was why everything seemed so different here.

14

WATCHING A CONTROVERSIAL 'SATANIC' FILM
1975

After deliberating about it with myself, I had gone to see the film that everyone was talking about, about a young girl who is exorcised. I went with Dora and Mum. It was R rated. I was also rather astonished when I read in a local newspaper that the film was going to be coming to a town quite nearby. That was close enough to go and see what the fuss was about; as I was fifteen I could see it with my parent or guardian, or with their permission. The film had been screened in Belfast, and other places too distant to travel to, and it would be here.

The screening was causing outrage. There were news reports of a picket and protest organised by a group which had campaigned against screenings across Britain, with a hymn-singing picket line, and a pastor outside the cinema, urging people to turn away, and handing out pamphlets with details of where to get spiritual help afterwards.

There had been news coverage following the film's release in England, about people fainting in the cinema.

There had been reports or rumours of teenage girls jumping off bridges after watching it. I thought that was tragic (if it was true). But, as a budding free thinker I thought I must see it. To decide what I thought. For some reason I assumed I would be immune to it affects (and special effects).

At school I tried to rally my friends to join me.

"Who wants to see it?" I asked.

"My parents wouldn't let me go," Margy said.

Bee and Tessa said nothing and seemed uninterested.

I asked Dora. "Do you want to watch it? Go on, be a devil."

All stupid bravado.

"Yes, I'll go. I'd like to see it," said Dora, in a cool, rational tone, as always. (Carly her younger sister was unwell, and not at school for a few weeks).

Mum said she would drive me and watch it with me and any of my friends who wanted to and whose parents allowed them. We arranged to collect Dora on our way and drive her home on our way back. (Dad was away on a work trip).

It was dark before five pm and by six thirty it was a cold night. We drove into town, parked and walked to the cinema. About twenty people in winter coats and scarves were standing with a pastor who was preaching against "the film of Satan..."

"It is the film of the Devil, do not ye enter the cinema, do nae go in!" He held aloft a crucifix and shouted dire warnings aimed at deterring people from stepping inside the building.

"Turn back now! All ye! Before it is too late!"

Others in the picket were handing out leaflets with advice on what to do in case of a crisis caused by watching the film, providing phone numbers, and details of the pastor's church, it was a mission which a local news reporter later wrote was to lead to a surge of conversions in the area.

I did not take any leaflets people tried to hand me. Instead, I walked with Dora and Mother, through the entrance to the cinema.

We took our seats, the lights dimmed, and the film began. I was comforted by the soundtrack from an album I had and liked. My bravado did not last. At the scene where the poor girl's head starts spinning around I whispered to Dora beside me:

"Do you want to go?"

"Yes," said Dora.

Mum, hearing us, stood up and we walked out quickly.

I resisted the leaflets on spiritual assistance being offered to us as we left the cinema after watching only the beginning of the film.

"That was pretty dreadful," I said, doing my best to be intellectual in the car as Mum drove through the dark countryside. "I read there was a controversy about how the music has been used in the film." I didn't exactly know what the controversy was about but I wanted to think about it in another way.

"Yes, I read that too," said Dora.

Images from the film replayed annoyingly in my mind. I did not want to admit it but I had been unnerved (rattled and scared out of my wits) by the too-realistic horror images.

We drove Dora to the front door of her farm house, waited until Carly opened it; Dora went inside, we waved, the door closed, and then we drove home.

That night I wanted to ask Lily if I could sleep in her room, but I didn't. I lay in bed. I couldn't sleep.

My thoughts of the film, and the fear it had made me feel, were joined by my dread about the impending dislocation of our lives that Dad had so casually introduced a couple of weeks ago telling us he was applying for jobs in other countries. We were going to be moving, yet again, and maybe that's what made me think about the next holidays. A more pleasant form of travelling lay ahead first.

I thought about the play which I was studying in English. It was a coincidence that on our next holiday, in the Easter break, we were going to be visiting Denmark and Sweden. We hoped to go to Kronborg Castle that the castle in the play was based on. To my joy and excitement, Margy was coming with us. Both sets of parents had consented to our requests. I tried to distract myself with thoughts of the holiday ahead. But it didn't exactly work.

I could hear creaks above me, in the attic, the dripping was starting up again.

I thought about the ghost of the deceased father in the play who is seen from the battlements of the castle.

In the play, the ghost is a harbinger of trouble, seeing it is a sign that things were going to go wrong, or more wrong than they already were. Our English teacher told my class there was speculation that the great playwright had written the play as a way of processing his grief at losing his son, who died at the age of eleven...That was sad, I thought.

Drip-drip-creak. The dripping was pattering and juddering all over the other side of the ceiling; the floor of the attic. It was making me scared.

I didn't like the dark.

I jumped up out of bed, hurried from my room into the hall. *Let there be light*. I flicked the switch. The hall lit up. I walked back into my room, leaving the door wide open, and got into bed.

The ghost was still in my mind. Gliding around the battlements of the castle walls and tower...

With a great effort of will, I told myself it was only a play, it was made up, it wasn't based on historical fact. And that film was of a fictional story. As I drifted into sleep I imagined travelling on the roads, as Dad drove us to Kronborg Castle, with Margy beside me. It never occurred to me that a ghost or two or more could have slipped into my imaginings and taken an invisible seat in the van, excited about the trip, as we all were. (A friendly ghost or two or more that would keep a low profile at first but would then become more present).

You see, I did what I could to help her and protect her, and I did protect her. Her new life was challenging, but nothing terrible happened to her then, in County Antrim. She found herself in dangerous situations, but was not physically injured, she was one of the lucky ones, and she rode her chestnut pony down country lanes and went out with her friends. Her life was nothing like mine. I watched her in incredulity. That girl and her friends do not have the manners I was brought up with. And that music she listens to is–interesting. But I liked her spirit, and her love of life. Of course, I could not protect her when she left here, and went off jaunting, and went on holidays...

15
ROAD TRIP TO SWEDEN AHEAD
EASTER HOLIDAY 1975

I found a booklet in a box of books in my study that must have been my mother's about significant days in Easter mystery mythology, and their meaning, which I jotted down, to write an assignment inspired by the English class Mythology project. Then I found to my surprise, later, that the days were apt in counterpoint for what happened on that fated road trip to Sweden, in the Easter school holidays and what happened then. It was a meaningful, albeit traumatic, way that I learnt more about the Easter mystery, so here I'll leave the names of some of the days.

16

DEPARTURE
PALM SUNDAY 1975

"It's okay to eat what we like, as it's not sweets," I reassured Margy and Lily at the surprise afternoon tea. For Lent, Lily and Margy and I had given up what we enjoyed most. I was looking forward to celebrating Easter day in the floating youth hostel which was to be our accommodation in Sweden. The Af Astrid was moored on a lake in the centre of Stockholm. In preparation for breaking my "fast" of forty days I had gradually filled a large plastic carrier bag with confectionery, Easter eggs, and chocolate bunnies that I'd saved up over Lent. Lily and Margy had also given up sweets and chocolate, but I had the most. Our bags of hoarded goodies were stored in our luggage packed in the back of the van, in the low cupboards made by Dad, under the covered foam mattresses made by Mum, that were now strewn with pillows, scatter cushions, and bedding, ready for the long drive ahead.

My family and Margy and I farewelled Margy's family, her mother and father, brother Sherry and younger sister Maud and a rather puzzled-looking Dusty and Jester who were holidaying with them. Sherry was grasping firmly onto Dusty's collar; Maud held Jester cat. They were assembling, smiling, in front of the front door of their house, as we climbed into the van. Margy, Sarah and I in the middle seat. Alex and Lily lay stretched out on the foam mattresses in the back.

I looked with mixed feelings at our beloved dog and cat with Margy's family.

Margy's mum hurried out of the front door towards us as I did up my seat belt. She was smiling and holding something.

"Take these for the trip, Isobel. Two apple cakes just out of the oven." She passed trays wrapped in tea towels through the side window. "Oh thank you, Gloria, and thank you for the splendid send off," said Mum in her warm smiling voice.

Margy's family had prepared a lavish repast of homemade cakes, scones and sandwiches which we had enjoyed when we arrived to collect Margy. Now, all of Margy's family were lined up outside their front door in a tableau. Gazing at Dusty and Jester with them I hid my dismay. For the sight was a portent of change, the bigger goodbye. Dad had applied for a job in Toronto. A job in Paris. And one in Australia. He had been offered all three and had to make his choice. Last week Dad had announced that he and Mum had decided he would take the appointment in Canberra, which began later this year. We would be moving to Australia this year. That was a prospect fraught with dread and fear for me. For Mum and Dad it was going 'home'. For me it was akin to leaving the known world and setting out to the farthest reaches of an unknown galaxy. Lily and I had wanted him to take the job in Paris, then we would not have been so far away from our friends, we'd be able to keep our beloved animals (maybe we could have bought a house outside Paris?) but my parents had decided to return home with us, their four children, after living and working in America and the UK for twenty years. And I was going to have to say goodbye to all that I knew and loved (apart from my family) again. I'd be going to my third secondary school in four years, each in a different country, all with different systems, that I was thrown into and expected to just pick myself up from and swim through it all doing wonderfully. What a joke. But I knew I had to try to be positive.

With goodbyes, smiles and waves, we drove down the lane

away from Margy's family's farm towards the road to the port, and the car ferry to Scotland.

After catching the ferry from Larne to Stranraer we stayed the night in a bed and breakfast house at the side of a country road and were back in our van by mid morning.

17

"POOR BEHAVIOUR GIRLS"
HOLY MONDAY 1975

It was a Monday. We motored across Scotland to the university where Dad was scheduled to deliver a presentation at a conference later in the afternoon.

Dad parked the van outside a historic granite building. We followed him, walking up a flight of granite steps and through large doors into an entrance foyer.

"Now everyone," Dad said with calm authority. "I'll be in the conference for an hour and a half. We'll all meet here, in this foyer, at five pm." His voice was firm, clear and reasonable as he explained: "We can't meet up later than that, as I have another meeting to attend at six pm, with Sister Joseph. You might remember her from the Donegal trip."

"What, you mean that nun?" said Lily loudly and rudely.

"Yes, she stayed with us, you remember," said Mum, supporting hopping Sarah who had hurt her foot.

Dad explained the itinerary. "We're following Sister Joseph's car to the college where I have a meeting I have to go to for an hour, then we'll all have dinner at the hall of residence where we'll be staying the night. We'll meet back here at five. On the dot. And remember, don't be late."

"Can me and Margy and Lily go for a bit of a walk along

72

the corridors to stretch our legs?" I asked.

"Margy, Lily and I," said my mother.

"Margy, Lily and I."

"Yes, you three can go for a walk, but you have to be back here at five. Roxanne, I'm putting you in charge."

"Okay Dad."

Lily placed her thumbs on either side of her face, waggled her fingers and stuck out her tongue at me behind Dad's back.

Margy and Lily and I spoke in low voices to each other; we had noticed an interesting sign on the wall. Margy was gesturing with a raised eyebrow, in a mimed question.

"We're just going for a bit of a walk around," I said to Mum, after Dad walked off. "We'll be back soon."

Margy, Lily and I set off, down a long corridor with a shiny floor. "There it is!" exclaimed Margy.

We hurried down the corridor and pushed open the glass panelled doors into a café, empty of patrons, where we made ourselves comfortable. As had become a tradition or a compulsion, when on holidays with saved pocket money, we set out to sample all the tempting foodstuffs on offer. As I bought my treats, I automatically added up the calories of my consumption.

One jam and cream doughnut, approximately 300; one slice of apple pie with cream, 450; one orange juice, 150; one oat cookie, 180–that was, what? In the gastronomic terms of my stomach it would all add up to feeling a bit queasy. My waistline straining at the waistband of my flared green loons.

We ate in a sugar coma, engrossed fully in the act of eating. All that mattered to us was that it was not confectionery, so that made it alright in Lent to eat as much as we could.

Time passed quickly in the café, as Margy and Lily and I

munched on. We ignored the disapproving eyes of attendants twirling tea towels behind the food counter.

"For God's sake girls, we have to go," Margy said bossily, as she wiped fake cream off her fingers with a paper serviette. "God, I'm stuffed! I don't know if I should have had that third éclair! Your dad said to meet him at five exactly."

"What's the time?" I asked, surreptitiously undoing the top button of my loons.

"It's five to five! We have to get back," Margy said. "Come on!"

"Five to five!" I stood up from my chair with difficulty.

"Just a minute," said Lily, eating a slice of marmalade cake. "I haven't finished …"

"I'm dying to go the loo," Margy said.

"So'm I, actually," I replied. "C'mon, let's quickly find the loos, there must be one on the way back…" We hurried off.

A few minutes later, Lily followed us. I could see her when I turned my head.

She was dawdling along the corridor way behind us.

Margy and I found a door emblazoned with a stick-woman icon.

I wondered why Lily did not seem in a good mood. Lagging behind, making us call out to her to catch up.

In the bathroom, Margy and I washed hands, peering into the mirrors. But Lily was still in a cubicle with the door locked.

"Come on Lily, hurry up, we're really late," I called to my sister cheerfully.

There was silence from behind the door.

"Lily, what are ye doin' in there," Margy admonished in her broad lough village accent, jokingly. There was no reply.

"Lily! Come on, Dad'll be mad!"

There was a groan, followed by a bang on the cubicle wall. Then the deliberately dramatic sound of a body sliding heavily down the wall, and slumping onto the floor. A swathe of long red-gold hair appeared, snaking out like seaweed from the gap under the cubicle door.

"LILY!" I shouted. "What are you doing?? We have to go!" No reply. Margy and I looked at each other with long-suffering, resigned expressions.

"Stop mucking around!" I commanded.

"She's lying on the floor in there," I added to Margy.

"C'mon Lily, ye gurn ye." Margy's words also met with no response. No matter what we said, nothing could disturb the silence or the hair spilling under the cubicle door.

"I think she's pretending to be dead: trying to make us feel sorry for her," I said. "But it's not going to work."

I raised my voice. "In fact, it's just pathetic. That's all it is, it just makes her look pathetic." But even these harsh words, not cruel but calculated to provoke a response, had no effect.

Realising there was nothing more we could do, and feeling apprehensive, I left the bathroom with Margy. We attempted to find our way to the entrance foyer. Corridors appeared to have turned into a mythological labyrinth.

After taking another wrong turn we finally arrived back at where we'd started from. Mum and Dad, Alex, and Sarah were standing in a tense group.

"Where have you been? What's happened?" said Dad in a tone of high alarm.

"We got lost," I said lamely. "Sorry, Dad…"

"You got lost!" he exclaimed. "It's nearly half past five!"

"Well Sister Joseph had to leave for the next meeting," he continued after a terrible silence in which I stared at the floor.

"She's given me directions and drawn a map showing how to get there, but I will have missed half of it. This is poor, very poor, girls."

"Sorry, Dad." I said again, feeling bad.

As he spoke these words, a new expression of alarm dawned on his face. He was not addressing enough girls.

"Where's Lily?" he demanded. "Where's your sister?"

"Er, she's still in the toilets," I said.

"Still in the toilets? Good grief. Could one of you girls go and get her, now!"

"Okay, I will." I ran back along the long corridor we'd just walked down what seemed like ages ago. How could we have been so light hearted?

When I reached the toilets, I pushed open the door. Lily was standing looking at her reflection in front of the mirror. With an expression of disdain and unconcern, my sister was finger-combing her red gold hair back and up, away from her face. Lily now enjoyed a striking resemblance to the figure in paintings by a group of late nineteenth-century painters Lily, Margy and I admired. It was a process of comparison, beloved of my mother's friends, and mine and Lily's friends, and their mothers, and even Margy, but tedious in its frequency and enthusiasm for me. "Oh Lily, oh Lily, you should be a model!"

The remarks began a few months back, after Lily had grown and lost almost a stone in weight, after a self-imposed regime of dieting and daily jogging on the spot in her bedroom, interspersed with running up and down the stairs from the ground floor hall to her bedroom and back, hundreds of times.

"Dad sent me to get you," I said. "C'mon, we're going. He said if you don't come now, you'll get left behind."

Without speaking, Lily followed me through the maze of

corridors to the family group.

When we reached the others, Lily simply tossed her head and hair back in a performance of pride, vanity, defensiveness and superiority and did not deign to speak. Was this all because Dad had put me in charge? I suspected it was. Dad turned without saying a word, and walked away, out the front doors. The rest of us followed to Bertie van, climbed in, and we drove in silence to the halls of residence where we were staying. We did not have dinner with Sister Joseph. We didn't even see her. We were too late. Dad missed his work meeting because of me, Margy and Lily. I was the only one of us who had apologised, it did not occur to me to suggest they apologise. I knew Lily would have ignored me; Margy might have thought it was funny.

18
THE VAN BREAKS DOWN
HOLY TUESDAY 1975

We left Glasgow at about nine-thirty the next morning. The plan was now to drive down to Southampton and from there to catch a ferry to Denmark then drive through Denmark and Sweden to Stockholm, where Dad had a conference to attend. But early that day something began to go wrong. Unpleasant fumes from the van's engine began to waft noxiously through the interior. I spotted a bag of bread rolls among some things on the floor under the glovebox. When I bit into one the toxic taste of carbon made me retch.

"Oh yuk! This is revolting. The whole bread roll tastes of fumes!" I spluttered.

"It's just the smell," Mum said evenly glancing at Dad as he drove. "Smell and taste are closely connected."

But taste or smell lingered, making me sick with a headache and nausea all day.

Under Dad's instructions, we opened all the windows. But other ill effects were, unaccountably, becoming manifest. The van, which had been motoring along at a steady seventy miles per hour, sitting on the motorway speed limit, was slowing down. Much as Dad tried to accelerate, the speed kept dropping from seventy to sixty-five, then down to sixty and fifty-five… We drove south through England at a declining pace in an increasing miasma of fumes inside the van, and road rage from outside the van, vented with vitriol by the beeping, swearing motorists who were held up in a queue behind us. A couple of times, going up hills, the van ground to a halt. We 'big kids,' as Mum called all those of us who were not Sarah, had to get out and push as my father attempted to restart the engine.

Sometimes kind motorists stopped and helped; each time Bertie re-started–but only just.

By the time we had reached Reading we were hours behind Dad's schedule, which was based on his meetings and the conferences he was speaking at. It was a holiday for us kids but for Dad it was a work trip which he was bringing his family on, so we could have Easter together. By the time Bertie had slowed to 35 mph, I was feeling nauseous. The speed kept dropping.

Dad greeted the first signs of mishap on the motorway with calm confidence. But after speaking with a mechanic on the trip southbound and attempting a minor repair that made no difference, he now changed tack.

"We'll have to get a new secondhand van in Southampton," Dad said calmly. Mum gazed at him wordlessly.

"We'll have to transfer our things into the new van, and

continue," he said.

By the time we reached Southampton the van was toiling at 10 miles per hour and making loud belching noises. All the windows that opened were open wide. Behind us, next to us, and in front of us, motorists were shaking their heads, waving fists, before, during and after noisily overtaking.

Our van didn't make it to the car yard. The family's trusty but rusty companion breathed a last shuddering fume-ridden gasp and conked out at the end of the street. It had been seven years since Dad first drove Bertie home, and the old van had a good few years behind him then. Everyone had to get out and walk the rest of the way to the car yard, and mechanics drove down to tow Bertie to his resting place.

Meanwhile, Dad was selecting a used van from the rows of vehicles.

The 'new' van was a different make, although it was cream, just like Bertie. We all worked hard transferring luggage from Bertie to the new van but none of us was in a frame of mind to come up with a new name. The new van was never named. It was known by us girls, contemptuously, as "the new van." Margy, Lily and I all agreed with each other. It was convention-al, lacking in character, unlike our comfortable, chubby-sided friend. What made us manufacture such a view I don't know. All I can do is acknowledge the three of us together were like that. (In my mind, I liken it to the pit ponies who after a life of pulling coal trolleys, blindfolded, underground in a coal mine, are finally taken to the surface of the earth, and set free in a field, in fresh air, and they canter and gallop, and buck and rear, like mad fillies and colts, in the joy of it; if living in the Troubles could be compared to life underground in a coal pit, on holiday we were, for a brief giddy time, set free. I knew how lucky I was, able to get away. But the giddiness of it could go to our heads, the three of us girls together.)

What was of more concern to Dad was the fact that he did not have the time or equipment to secure the custom benches he'd built for the back of Bertie, which he now had to transfer. Lining each side, they'd doubled as storage spaces for food and travel supplies; on our road trips they were covered with light-weight boards and ingenious foldable covered foam mattresses that Mum made; strewn with cushions and duvets these made a bed upon which passengers could recline in comfort. But now Dad could only prop up not bolt down the benches. Another difference was that whilst it had side windows in the front section, the new van had no side windows in the back so whomever was reclining in the back could only see out by looking forwards, lying on their front or side or looking through the back door windows (which was very different to Bertie's windows in the middle seat sliding side doors and back). It was more claustrophobic for those lying in the back.

"We have to work quickly, everyone," Dad kept urging us. "We're already running late for the ferry. It leaves at five pm."

He glanced at his watch. "Cripes! Jump in! If we're lucky we'll just make it!"

The big kids and the little kid scrambled to take their new places on the middle bench seat (Alex, Sarah, me) or dive over it and lie down on the mattresses and cushions in the back (Margy, Lily). Mum and Dad slid open the driver and front passenger doors and stepped up to their new seats. Dad was the driver. They did not share the driving on our road trips. Those with seat belts did them up.

Then, with a confident roar, the new van took off.

The streets were clogged. We stopped in a stationary jam. As time lengthened, Dad's mood of competent optimism, which had lifted everyone's spirits, seemed to shift gears downwards. At least he'd stopped sighing with gritted teeth. Now in the new van his mood seemed more to be fatalistic humour.

His thumbs tapped the steering wheel as we were halted by yet another red traffic light.

"Oh my God, we're not going to make it," Lily said.

"We will make it, of course we'll make it," I replied as the new van started to move. After what seemed like an eternity we broke free of the traffic jam, but only to join the tail end of another column of crawling cars.

By the time we'd managed to idle across town, there was an air of almost hysterical hilarity in the van.

Driving almost at the speed limit we screeched towards the harbour. Pulling up on the wharf we were just in time to see– the car ferry heading out into the channel.

"Damn," Dad said. Things were not well. "We'll just have to stay overnight and catch the ferry tomorrow. I'll go and sort it out. Wait here, everyone." Dad climbed out of the new van and walked towards the terminal building on the wharf.

He returned, seemingly back to his usual good spirits.

"We'll stay the night here in a B and B, then we'll get the ferry tomorrow," Dad said to Mum as we young people, the audience, avidly craned necks and ears their way.

"It's not too bad, we can get the five pm ferry, it just means we're running twenty-four hours behind our schedule. We'll have less time to spend in Denmark and driving up through Sweden. That's all."

"Alright, darling," said Mum, supportive as always.

We stayed that night in a small, cramped Bed and Breakfast.

19

TRAGIC NEWS ON THE FERRY
HOLY WEDNESDAY 1975

We had the day to get through in Southampton. We walked around the town centre and the shops, had a picnic lunch in a park, and were in the van at the head of the queue, ready to board the ferry when the gates opened.

I and Margy and Lily were all about to explore the ferry and find the cafeteria.

There was a crackle from above. An announcement came over the Public Address speakers.

"Professor Bergson please go to the Registrar. Professor Marcus Bergson. Would Professor Marcus Bergson please go to the Registrar. Professor Marcus Bergson to the Registrar.

Paging Professor Marcus Bergson. Would Professor Marcus Bergson please go to the Registrar." Enunciated a mellifluous female voice about twenty or thirty times.

"What's your dad done now?" Margy sly-boots whispered to me.

"Oh darling," Mum said, making concerned noises, as Dad headed off.

An hour or so later Mum approached Margy, Lily and me. We were sitting at a table in the cafeteria, surrounded by an array of snacks and treats with an intriguing Scandinavian theme.

Mum looked worried as she walked up, and stood in front of us. I observed she was dressed quite smartly in her brown wool coat over a green lightweight suit, hair in a chignon. She was wearing pink lipstick which looked freshly applied. There was a pause as we waited for her to speak.

Why wasn't she saying anything?

"Pa's died," Mum said.

"What?" The three of us exclaimed in shocked unison.

"What do you mean?" I stammered.

"Dad's father's died. That's what the announcement was."

"Oh no," I groaned.

"Oh God," said Lily.

"Oh dear," replied Margy anxiously.

Mum hurried away looking concerned and subdued.

I had met Pa and Nana in Sydney. We'd met when Mum took Lily, Alex and I to Australia for a few months when I was a young child. It was before Sarah was born. Dad went to India for work and Mum took us three little kids to Sydney where we stayed with Grandmother and Grandfather, in their house overlooking a gully where she grew up. We visited Nana and Pa and stayed there at their house in Crows Nest where Dad had lived when he was a student at university where he and Mum had first met. What I remembered about Pa was that he was a kindly man who made himself popular with us by giving us wheelbarrow rides, pushing his shrieking scions around the lawn in a large wooden barrow.

Lily and I had sometimes asked Mum about our relatives in Australia and she would reply in carefully guarded grown-up terms. But she was more expansive telling us colourful stories about when she was a girl growing up in a house above a gully. A word that intrigued me. Dad did not talk much about his childhood. He did tell us where he had lived once, in a mining town in the outback, water was brought into town on a train.

And he did tell us a story about a time when he was doing his military service, and driving through an outback town, he picked up a man who was hitchhiking who implored him not to drive down a particular street, as the man said there was a ghost down there! And was there, was there a ghost there? We children clamoured to know.

Dad said well, he didn't know, but the man had certainly seemed to think so; and as the man was so agitated, Dad had detoured and not driven down that street.

On that visit, Nana had shown me drawings and paintings Dad had made when he was a boy. Nana kept them in a chest of drawers, others were framed and hung on the walls.

I remember Pa. We kids are screaming, laughing, clinging to the sides of the wheelbarrow, as it veers from side to side, yet my younger brother and sister and I feel safe in the hands of the gruff man who's running around and around the lawn, pushing us before him in a crazy loop, whose sense of connection to us is released in this moment. The sky is dazzlingly blue, infinitely lighter than it is at home. Sunlight irradiates bushes, trees and flowers. Each short stiff blade of grass casts a sharp shadow. Lily, Alex and I crushed together in the barrow, holding tight onto the sides, screaming in delight as Pa runs, pushing us. Until he stops, and he tips us out in a shrieking laughing heap. Onto scratchy grass that smells of eucalyptus and sunshine. Screaming for more.

I didn't know what to say when Lily, Margy and I met up with Dad later, sitting in one of the lounge areas with Mum. He wasn't saying anything. As he had not often spoken about his family, I thought that must mean I was not meant to speak about Pa. Mum didn't give out any clues. After a short uncomfortable time, Lily said: "Shall we go and have a look around?" and Margy, Lily and I wandered away. I felt sad but I did not say it and kept it to myself. It felt clumsy. But I thought it was all I could do.

Margy, Lily and I mooched around, exploring options for night-time entertainment in a desultory fashion. We found a bar with a disco. We stood at the side of a dance floor strobed with pink and green lights for a short while. Margy and Lily danced but there weren't any eligible looking fellas there, they agreed. And it didn't feel right. Thinking and talking like that. It felt wrong. We walked around, not doing anything much.

"I'm going out on deck for a little while," I said. "I won't be long."

I felt like being alone. I walked along the cold and windy deserted boards. I leaned against the railing at the front of the ferry staring into the black night. The furious cold wind tore at my long thick hair. Black water churned and frothed into white horses beneath the carving motion of the boat. Black water rushed into the black sky. Blackness stretched all around. The freezing wind lashed at my pale skin. My ancestors on Dad's father's side came from Sweden. They must have rowed to England in the opposite direction to the one we were heading in; they came over in longboats in the Viking invasion in the eighth century. This was a trip, our family's first, back to an ancestral homeland. How strange and sad that it should be accompanied by the death of my grandfather.

I shivered suddenly. What was that I heard, travelling on the biting wind? A high-pitched singing. My ears strained to follow but I couldn't catch the sounds. It felt and sounded as if there was something cold, foreign, and frightening out there in the night calling me. I could almost hear it, but it was out of reach, whipping at my ears. The ferry pitched from side to side, up and down, on the wild waves.

The wind held me in its grasp. I was caught for I know not how long. In the black plunging wilderness of the North Sea at night. I couldn't move.

I became aware of myself. What was I doing here? I turned and hurried down the deck, wrestling with the wind buffeting me sideways. Pushing the door handle against the tremendous force trying to sweep me away, into the waves. I pushed open the metal door. Forward into the Viking Queen's interior, into the comforting illusion of stable land.

20

FREEZING IN COPENHAGEN
MAUNDY THURSDAY 1975

We sailed into Copenhagen on a crisp clear early morning and drove to a youth hostel in town. We arrived there in time to have breakfast. Margy, Lily and I performatively expressed our delight with breakfast at the youth hostel. But my performance, at least, was forced. Trying to act as if things had not gone wrong. But this felt wrong to me. The youth hostel breakfast was provided, like a hotel breakfast. Not a greasy fry up, or packet of cornflakes, such as we'd had in Bed and Breakfasts at other times and places. Here, breakfast was literally a smorgasbord. Of fresh fruit salad, muesli, yogurt, cheese, cold meats for the non-vegetarians and rye bread. Real coffee and tea. Outside, snow began to fall. It whirled past the windows.

"Better eat up everyone, a full stomach is the best way to keep out the cold," Dad said gamely.

Dad still hadn't mentioned Pa's death. He was quieter and more subdued. I lowered my voice and my eyes every time I passed him, in what I knew was a clumsy attempt to indicate my sympathy. I was uncomfortably aware my whole response was inadequate. With no direction or pointers from the adults, and having had no experience of anyone dying in our family to learn from, I didn't know what to do. Only months before we moved to Australia we had lost Pa. It was tragic.

Dad's advice was sound because breakfast turned out to be the highlight of our time there. We spent the day walking around Copenhagen. I sang along with Margy, Lily and Alex, the song from the black-and-white film set in Copenhagen we'd watched on television. What was it called? No-one could remember. We were trying to keep up our spirits and act more appropriately for a school holiday. Shouldn't we all have been in mourning, I think so now. Was our behaviour wrong? Out of kilter. What else could we have done?

The streets and air were freezing. It was the coldest Easter for fifty years I was informed by a young man with a Scottish accent. Snow was whirling. Mantling pavements, parks, roads. Snowdrifts creeping up sides of buildings. Canals were freezing over. Snow white streets were treacherous and icy.

Margy, Lily and I were wearing platform shoes that leaked. Our feet cold as the ice and snow we crept over, trying not to slip and fall, as we explored the city.

Finally, in despair, by a frozen canal, I stopped Dad who was forever leading the way. Almost crying with pain and cold, I told him we girls could not go on. Then we saw Dad's capable side. "Don't worry," he said. "We just need to fix things up." Producing some plastic bags, like a conjurer, from his pockets he made each of us girls in turn take our feet out of our shoes. He then carefully wrapped our sopping wet icy feet in plastic bags. Then he helped each of us replace our feet in our shoes.

"There you are. How does that feel?" he asked when he had

tended to all three sets of feet, in turn.

"Fine!" we chorused happily. And indeed, it did.

Then off we set again, re-committed to the cause–of team spirit, trying to enjoy life as it comes no matter what. No one said anything about Pa. I knew it was because we had to keep going without thinking or dwelling too much. At least that's what I thought it all meant we had to do.

After this Lily bought a pair of clogs with leather uppers, and wooden soles. She also bought a black, woollen zippered jacket. Everyone in the markets seemed to be wearing them. Later I wished I had bought one too with my pocket money. I bought a pair of high heeled clogs made of leather and wood, with brass studs affixing the leather to the wooden sole, and a seam up the front. Not to wear here in this weather, but for when we returned home.

21
SWEDISH SNOWSTORM
GOOD FRIDAY 1975

The next morning, after breakfast, we packed up and got into the van and Dad drove us out of Copenhagen. It was still snowing hard. Dad said there was not enough time to go on the Tour of the castle I'd wanted to go on. Nor even to have a walk around. And now we had to drive to the port.

At midday we boarded the car ferry. This carried us in little time across the narrow stretch of choppy grey water called the Sound to Sweden. It was snowing.

We bought some fresh food items at a shop near the wharf. "We'll have lunch on the way at a Viking settlement site," said Dad, driving through the building storm.

We ate our rye bread, cheese and fruit in a wooden picnic shelter at the site of the long ago Viking settlement. While we were eating our sandwiches, an ominous howling wind drove madly whirling snow hither and thither.

"Looks like it's setting in," said Dad.

Alex ran off laughing and disappeared behind the shelter.

As Margy, Lily and I got up to walk to the van he pelted us with snowballs. All three of us girls returned fire, or rather ice and snow. Scooping up white handfuls with numb red fingers, clumping the flakes into snowballs.

"Take that!" Hurling them at Alex who fired back before running to the van which Dad was revving up, Mum beside him, ready for the next leg of the road trip. Sarah was already on the middle seat. We all climbed into our places (which for Margy and me, this time, was the mattresses, to recline). Dad released the handbrake, pushing down his foot on the accelerator, and onwards we sped beneath lowering clouds. Into the storm. That snowball fight stands out as one of the last scenes of normality, of me in my old life, that I remember.

And the snow it did verily fall. And the wind it did roar.

We stayed that night in a youth hostel in Ljungby.

22

HOLY SATURDAY 1975

If Denmark was freezing, Sweden was Polar. Sweden was deeper snow. Sweden was so white and snow-covered I couldn't see Sweden. All I could see was ice, snow, and blizzard. We were on a highway driving to Linköping. We were supposed to be staying the night at Jönköping, following Dad's itinerary. We had arrived at the youth hostel as the sky darkened, night was falling and the blizzard was setting in. But when we pulled up outside the tall terrace house, it was forbiddingly silent and dark. Not a light on in the building.

"This can't be right," said Dad. He sounded impatient and uncharacteristically irritable. The drive from where we'd stayed the previous night had been longer than he had planned, many hours in worsening conditions. Who would have known that the weather at Easter would be like this? My parents had not given us any indication we would be holidaying in a blizzard. (They obviously had had no idea). Ridiculously, I had thought it would be springtime weather. Because it was, well, Spring. It was irritating me. The further north we travelled the worse it became; it felt like we were entering the depths of perpetual winter.

In the front seat, Mum pored over the International Youth Hostel Association Handbook.

"No 32. This is the right address," she said, unflustered.

She paused. "Ah, what's this … Closed between September and May…" Her voice remained calm.

"What?" said Dad, voice rising with emotion. "How come you didn't see that before?"

"It's in very small print, darling," Mum said in a reassuring tone. "It's almost impossible to see it."

"Give me the book," Dad said brusquely. There was silence in the middle seats and back as Margy, Lily, Alex, Sarah and I all listened to the tension in the front. It had been a long drive through falling snow. I'd been looking forward to arriving at the youth hostel and having a shower before dinner, dreaming of hot water powering onto the nape of my neck. Outside, the air was cold enough to freeze my breath into frost.

"We'll have to drive on to Linköping, there's a youth hostel there," Dad said.

Mum turned and looked at him steadily. "Yes, darling."

Snow whirled against the van windows.

"How far away is it?" I asked from the middle seat.

"About one hundred and thirty kilometres up the highway," Dad replied.

"About eighty miles," Mum translated.

"How long 'til we're there?" yelled Lily lying on the cushions with Margy beside her.

"It should take an hour. We should just make it by eight. That's the closing time for signing in." Even Dad's voice was icy as he turned the key in the ignition.

The snow pounding the windscreen was driving faster and more furiously. Dad who was usually so sure about everything, then said he didn't know how to drive out of town because he couldn't see any street signs as everything was covered in snow. No people on streets covered in deepening silent drifts. It was like the end of the world.

And then.

"There's someone," said Mum. A hunched man in a dark overcoat was hurrying. Dad drove up alongside him to ask the way. But instead of stopping and helping us the man seemed frightened and sped off. Margy and Lily in the back started laughing.

Dad wound down his window.

"Excuse me," he called again. The man hurried away, head down, it looked as if he was moving as fast as he could go into the blizzard. Margy and Lily lying in comfort laughed hysterically. It was all making me feel bad tempered. The snow. The night. Missing out on, or at least postponing, a hot shower.

I remembered there were batches of Margy's mum's home

made apple cake in the back of the van. I hadn't eaten all day in self-imposed penance for eating too much the day before, starting with my breakfast at the youth hostel in Copenhagen. In addition to that, now it was Easter eve. Tomorrow would be Easter–the end of Lent. I would, at last, be able to tuck into Easter eggs and confectionery which I had saved up in the forty days and nights and brought with me. Another way of thinking about it all was I'd 'sweets-fasted' to prepare my stomach for the sugar onslaught of breaking my 'fast' on Easter Day. So had Margy and Lily. To make it all the more enjoyable and meaningful, I decided to defer gratification and save the apple cake until tomorrow.

Dad sighed with frustration. He was trying to find his way out of the deserted city by road signs which were impossible to spot as the snow blizzard increased in intensity. Visibility was reducing. The white buildings grew further apart. Snow-clad forests loomed each side of the highway. The map was easier to see than the actual streets, and after looking at it, Dad had managed to drive out of the city. All I could discern through the white-out and the falling darkness beyond the van window was that the houses and city streets were behind us.

A single wide straight motorway connected the two cities. Our van appeared to be the only vehicle on the road.

Dad pushed his foot down on the accelerator, he was determined to get us all to the hostel before it closed.

The highway passed through conifer forests alongside Lake Vättern. A vast, eerie frozen lake. I imagined a giant made of snow and ice attacking headlights, slamming into the slushy windscreen wipers juddering beneath their load. Visibility had reduced to nothing.

"Like in a film," I thought. (But which one, I didn't know).

It was warm in the van. I had taken off my shoes and socks, my jeans were rolled to mid calf; my feet and calves were bare.

Dad was driving fast. There was something strange and not quite right about it all I thought. Were we not going too fast for these atrocious conditions? It was impossible to see in the driving snowstorm, and the highway was deep in slippery icy snow.

"Slow down!" Lily shouted. That was another shock. Never before had I heard her challenging Dad's authority. She was commanding him to behave in a different way. He ignored her. I was still sitting in the middle seat in between Alex and Sarah in the blizzard. Everything was strange, shocking. This situation, in the van. That we were driving, now, in a blizzard, so fast. That Dad did not seem to be able to hear, or even to be here. There was a weird unreality to it all, like in a nightmare. I was not wearing a seat belt. There were only two seat belts on the middle seat. Which Alex and Sarah had strapped over their bodies. I had thought it was better that they had the seat belts as they were younger than me.

The feeling of urgency in the new van made me very alert. I'd wanted to have a better view. I had been lying in the back on the mattresses, blankets and quilts with Lily and Margy. I had climbed over to the middle seat where I was now sitting. I couldn't see much through the space in between my parents in the front seats. So I decided to move further forward. I wanted to see as much as it was possible to see.

I clambered through a gap between the backs of the driver seat and front passenger seat until I was sitting between Mum and Dad. There was no third seat belt in between the driver and passenger seats, I perched on the vinyl-covered bench seat section between the proper seats. It wasn't a proper seat at all.

Now I had a better view, but what could I see? The blizzard. The windscreen with battalions of fresh snow flakes mashing into slush, the windscreen wipers straining, swish-swishing, to clear the snow, as we hurtled into the encroaching unknown.

I couldn't really see anything through the furiously whirling raging snow.

Visibility was reduced to nothing beyond the windscreen.

I could see my parents, if I glanced at them.

Dad was driving as if his hands were frozen to the wheel, an expressionless look on his face. He seemed unapproachable, angry. Mum was staring ahead into the night.

I had a sudden vision of an artwork I saw only in my mind. A girl crouched kneeling, forehead on knees, curled up like an embryo, on top of a dark hill, in the light of the moon. It was an ethereal image. As if she was waiting to be born. A vision.

I glanced at the speedometer.

The red needle was hovering.

Dad was driving at about seventy miles per hour.

"Don't you think we're going too fast?" It was Margy's turn to call from the back. Dad ignored her.

"SLOW DOWN!" shouted Margy and Lily together.

Dad ignored them.

"Yeah, slow down, Dad," I joined the chorus. "We're going too fast for this weather. Does it really matter if we're not there by eight?"

Dad ignored me.

It was as if he had not even heard. I was sitting right next to him. I could see what he looked like. An impenetrable mask. Staring ahead. He kept driving at relentless speed. A feat that Bertie could never have achieved in the best of conditions. But this new van was of a different calibre. Efficient and capable of far higher speeds. Dad was determined to get us to the youth hostel in time.

Suddenly, the van skidded. Adrenalin shrieked through my nerve endings, everything lurched. The van swerved for twenty or thirty or a hundred feet. Two hundred feet. Or more. I had no idea. A long terrifying zigzagging skid.

Dad brought the van back under control.

"We must have hit some black ice," Dad's first words since we left the city.

"Black ice, what's that?" Alex asked from the middle seat.

"Ice that's below the surface of the snow," Mum's tone was incongruously reassuring. It all seemed surreal.

What was going on? Could this be really happening? I had a vertiginous feeling as if I was on the edge of a new reality. At the brink of unreality. Or was it the other way round.

Despite the skid, Dad didn't reduce his driving speed.

He was determined to get there.

"SLOW DOWN!" Lily and Margarita shouted in unison from the back again.

"Can't you go a bit slower, please Dad, surely this is much too fast!" I implored. Surely this was not right? In these conditions. Skidding on the black ice was a warning. The van was a container made of metal and we were fallible, soft, flesh-and-blood beings inside it. My confidence in my father's judgment was–shockingly–starting to waver.

Did it matter what time we reached the youth hostel?

Surely all that mattered was that we got there alive.

Couldn't we have pulled over and slept in the van until the blizzard passed? But where? In a snowdrift?

Dad paid no attention to words begging him to slow down.

Dad gave no indication he could hear what we were saying

and shouting: SLOW DOWN!

It was as if Dad had become sealed in a bubble and couldn't see or hear anyone.

He was the driver. And he was ignoring us.

My eyes were fixed on the speedometer wavering at seventy-three mph.

We hit another patch of black ice. At least that must have been what happened. The van skidded wildly. This was faster than anything I'd felt before. The worst feeling in the world. Zigzagging out of control, across the highway in the blizzard.

I could see Dad's face, as he gripped the steering wheel, he looked determined, as if battling an enemy, he was fighting for control, then his features contorted and froze in a grimace of horror I shall never forget.

Dad had lost control.

This time he would not win. The forces of fate, of life and death, had taken over.

We were going to crash.

We were going–

We were–

This is it.

I'm going to die.

Now I'm going to find out what it means *TO DIE!*

My last thought, as we skidded at helter-skelter speed, was that I wanted to convey to all the people in the van, my family, my close friend, that I loved them. I'M SORRY I'VE BEEN SUCH A BAD TEMPERED BITCH LATELY.

I LOVE YOU! I will love you forever.

I wasn't wearing a seat belt.

Now, like an aeroplane gathering speed, leaving the ground

with an impossible lurch, the van leapt and flew upwards from the snowbound road.

I flung my arms out on either side of me to stop my parents falling forward.

We hurtled into the unknown.

I blacked out. Lost consciousness. Afterwards I could never remember the van flipping through the air.

I opened my eyes. I was crushed, upside down. Lily's voice boomed.

"We're alright, everyone, we're alright. Don't worry, we're alright."

Screaming and crying.

Lily's voice tore at my ears.

I was crushed. Curled up on the ceiling. Ahead, I could see out through the windscreen.

On the snow. The glow of a red-orange light.

Fire!

My third moment of mortal terror. I was about to be incinerated.

When the father of a girl from my class at school had taken us to a local stock car race I'd watched stock cars crashing horrifically. After crashing, the cars exploded into fireballs as the spilt petrol ignited. Or did I see it on TV?

Now it was going to happen to me. To all of us.

Sobbing and screaming roared in my ears.

I was trapped or squashed against the ceiling. Either side of me, my parents dangled suspended from their seat belts, their limbs waving, like insects on their backs. With no seatbelt to strap me in, hold me in place, I was the only one able to move freely. I was the only one able to do anything.

Claustrophobia rose up, into wild panic. I had to get out! I clambered forward and pounded the windscreen with my fist. Blood ran from my knuckles. The windscreen wouldn't break.

Dad pounded at the windscreen with his fist. It didn't break. I looked over Mum towards the side window. Saw the window winder. I reached, grasped it, wound backwards, upside down. I rolled the glass, rolled it all the way...

Escape! Driven by sheer panic, like a wild animal, with no thought but to escape.

I slid over Mum and out the window, faster than I've ever moved in my life, into a snow drift. It felt faster than I'd ever moved in my life.

My life–what a precious gift.

The sweet air–I was breathing! I slid into snow and stood up. My feet and lower legs bare. I was standing in a snow drift but felt no cold. It was like being reborn.

I must have walked up a hill through deep snow.

Terror rose up in me like vomit.

The others. The others.

Were they alright?

I could see the van submerged in a snowdrift.

Upside down.

I was in total shock.

A vehicle had stopped. I could see and hear two men, two figures in dark clothes leaping and bounding down the snow slope to our van, shouting. Arms held high; they ran downhill through the snow.

The men were wrenching open the back doors. Pulling out one then the other, Lily and Margy, staggering onto their feet, dazedly in the snow drift. (Later, Lily told me they had been smothered and were suffocating under the bedding and all the things that fell on top of them as the benches weren't secured; the two men reached them and pulled them out just in time).

The van lying in the snowdrift, a twisted hulk of metal.

Not far from the van was the frozen lake. Ahead were snow covered conifer trees, a pine forest…I couldn't look at it. The others. The others. Were they all alright? I was terrified. The men were shouting, pulling open doors. People were climbing out or being helped. Alex. Sarah. Mum. Dad. Everyone. We were all alive. It was a miracle, comprised of several miracles. First that we did not fly off the road and crash through the icy lake, instead just missing it, as we had left the road at what was one of the few places where there was a shallow indent of land, which was filled with a snow drift deep enough to cushion the impact (or the van would have exploded). Then that we did not hit one of the tall fir trees I could see in what looked like a forest next the lake, covered in snow, which the van missed too. Then, that the men had been out driving in the blizzard too, and had seen me and then the crashed van, and had been willing and able to help us, and who saved all of the others by wrenching open doors and pulling them out or helping them out. Then that someone somehow called emergency services, how I have no idea, it was out in the wilderness, maybe they drove to the nearest settlement, or maybe it was someone who lived not far away.

And the orange glow on the snow was not what I thought, the start of a fire that would consume us all, but the headlight. Or else we would have been incinerated.

All these miracles together, of luck, kindness and competence, saved our lives. I would realise later.

But at that point I was standing in utter shock in the snow. As I watched the scene unfold, the men pulling out Lily and

Margy, then Mum and Dad and Sarah and Alex.

Everything was fragmented, floating away.

Margy, staggering through deep snow up the slope towards me. We hugged, sobbing, as if we couldn't let go.

Someone led us to a parked car and helped us inside.

I heard words. "Waiting for the police, sit here, wait here…" Everything was whirling past me in a dizzy rush. People were speaking in English with Swedish accents.

I have no idea how long I sat with Margy in the car, our arms around each other, we were sobbing uncontrollably. Gradually our sobbing diminished. Police cars arrived. Sirens wailing. Lights flashing; an ambulance stopped. An ambulance man opened the car door, peered in at us, they said something in Swedish, closed the door.

A police officer opened the door. "You come with us now, we take you to the youth hostel," he said in English. Carefully, Margy and I got out and walked to the police car through the snow. My feet and calves were bare.

I couldn't feel any coldness. I could not feel a thing.

The police drove too quickly for my shocked nerves, down the snowbound highway. "Er, please could you slow down," I implored. The speed of the vehicle was terrifying me.

The blizzard had eased. But it was still snowing. The others were going in another car, Mum had said something about it, but I hadn't heard her properly. All I knew was that Margy and I were in a police car, we were alive, being driven through the snow, and I was terrified.

"Please could you slow down?" I asked a second time. They didn't seem to understand. (No doubt they had chains on their car tyres or some other safety features for the weather).

At the youth hostel, the proprietors were waiting for us. A middle aged couple. Margy and I stepped out of the car. The others materialized behind us; they must have been following down the highway. The proprietors did not speak English and we could not speak any Swedish. The police officers and proprietors spoke briefly to each other, it was all far beyond words. After goodbyes and with our heartfelt mortal thanks, the police officers departed. How could we ever thank those who helped us, who had saved us, whose names and faces we would never know. They were unsung, unknown heroes. Supper had been prepared by the kindly proprietors. A selection of cold meats, rye bread and cheeses spread across a table in an empty dining room. I ate but couldn't taste the food. I had no sensation of hunger or thirst either.

We were shown to the rooms where we were to spend the night. Lily, Margy, Sarah and I were sharing a dormitory room of bunk beds.

We didn't ever talk about it, really. We referred to it as 'The Accident'. As I remember. Not much later, Mum said to me and Lily that her last thought as the van skidded off the road towards the frozen lake was: 'I'm glad we are all going to die together'. Thinking about this, many years later, I think about Margy who Mum included as one of 'us'. But Margy was part of her family, who certainly would not have felt the same way as my beloved Mum if we had not been so miraculously lucky.

23

EASTER SUNDAY 1975
THE RESURRECTION

I woke and sat up. Opened my eyes. I was alive. But everything seemed strange, as if the day was muffled around its edges, and snow covered everything. I couldn't think about what had happened.

"It's Easter," said Lily in a desultory tone.

I wanly tried to smile.

"Let's go and have breakfast," said Margy.

"A headache?"

"No, breakfast. Easter breakfast," said Margy.

We walked out, looking for the dining room. It was a large, whitewashed hall with blonde pine floors and tables. Breakfast was a lavish healthy smorgasbord. Yogurts, muesli, wholemeal bread, jams, meats, eggs, cheese, orange juice, filter coffee or tea.

We three older girls joined a queue of tall, healthy-looking people. Despite my state, I stole small glances at my fellows, possible relatives in ancestry. I served myself a bowl of muesli, yogurt and fruit.

Margarita, Lily and I sat down and ate. As we were eating, Dad walked in. He had been at the wreckers yard, where the van had been towed.

"Happy Easter everyone," he said, approaching the table.

"Happy Easter," we chorused without conviction.

"I've got something for you, when you've finished eating, in your room," he said, as if it was very important.

When we'd finished (and no one felt like second helpings), we returned to our rooms. Dad to his and Mum's and Sarah's.

Alex had slept in another one. Dad walked in.

He was holding a white plastic bag.

"Here you are, I brought this for you," he said to me.

He passed me the bag.

I opened it.

Inside something looked horribly familiar. Purple foil, gold foil, silver foil.

Gingerly, I extracted a shard of chocolate to which clung shreds of shiny foil. Incongruous festive scraps. The bag was filled with smashed pieces of the confectionery we'd saved to eat on Easter day. Today. Dad had salvaged the broken pieces from the frozen wreckage.

"Oh, thanks Dad," I said, trying to sound enthusiastic, but not knowing why I was bothering. I was filled with visceral revulsion.

Dad was standing expectantly before me, as if the broken chocolate Easter egg would somehow make everything alright.

I tried eating a little piece. It was frozen. The jagged edges stuck in my throat.

Food of the dead... the words went through my mind. After that day I would never want to eat chocolate again.

"It's stopped snowing," said Dad brightly, as if that would cheer us all up.

Dad said we had to go to the wreckers yard to salvage our belongings.

"The van is a write-off," he said.

The plan was that Dad would hire another van to transport all of us to Stockholm. He said that we must help. Then Dad left to hire a van. Mum said she'd better ring Margy's parents, to let them know what had happened: our van had crashed in a snowstorm and we were all alright.

After Dad left, I wandered into the room where Mum was sitting on the bed, next to piles of things on the bed.

"What's happening?" asked Lily.

"Well, Daddy's going to rent another van. We're going to drive to Stockholm. We'll stay on the yacht for five days, as we planned. Daddy will go to his conference here. Then Daddy must go to his work in France. He will fly there on his own. The rest of us will travel by train back down through Sweden, through Germany, the Netherlands, Belgium, to France where we'll meet Daddy…we'll be staying at the youth hostel there as planned. Daddy will hire another van in France…"

As Mum was talking, I wandered into the hallway. I didn't feel well.

Everything seemed mechanical, slow.

Now, absently my fingers ran over the foil-covered shards. Lost in non-thought, I lifted a handful of broken pieces from my pocket. I peeled back the foil and took a bite. I munched on it mechanically not even aware of what I was doing.

My head was throbbing and I had a weird, thick, muffled sensation as if the world around me was surrounded by muzzy cotton wool, a thick blanket of snow. The dazzling whiteness of the snow outside all the windows hurt my eyes and made me shiver. I wandered into the women's bathroom and moved towards the mirror. What I saw shocked me.

I had a black eye. My left eye was swollen to a slit. The skin around it was puffy, shiny, vividly coloured in shades of dark purple and puce, toning into violent raspberry and yellow.

"A classic shiner," I might have expected Alex to say but no-one commented on it. No-one mentioned it and no one looked at it. Even the person from the ambulance at the crash had not seemed to notice it. (Although it was dark in the car).

Dazedly, I wandered into the hallway. The others were all in Mum and Dad's room, talking and eating bits of chocolate.

"No thanks, I can't," I said to Lily passing me a spiky piece of broken Easter egg.

Time passed in a kind of haze. Then Dad returned with the new, new van. Oddly, it was also off-white or cream-coloured, like Bertie and the last one.

"Come on everyone," he said. "We'll set off from here now. First, we're going to the wrecker's yard and taking our things out of the van. We'll transfer them into the rental van. Then we'll come back here and pick up your mother and Sarah and leave for Stockholm."

Lily, Alex, Margy and I followed Dad walking out of the youth hostel down wooden front steps into knee deep snow, a path had been cleared, dug to the car park area. The world was blinding in its dazzling whiteness. Above us the cloud-covered low sky was filling ominously with more snow, waiting to fall. Alex threw a snowball at Lily.

I shivered as I climbed into the rental van. It was literally squeaky clean. It smelled of thick clear plastic. But questions of aesthetics hardly seemed to matter now. It was not our van, it was hired to take us only to Stockholm—that is, if everything went according to plan.

That was when I realized with a sudden sense of enormity, that I could never take the certainty of things going to plan for granted ever again. Who could ever know what was going to happen next? All I knew with any certainty was that no-one could ever know the certainty of anything.

It was as if... I was struggling to think. Everything was so white, blanketed in snow. We pulled up outside the wreckers' yard and I slid open the van door. I was in the middle seat. It was like opening the door of a freezer. The light outside was harsh, cold, dazzling. My eyes stung, smarting from the glare. A few flakes of snow whirled dismally, abysmally, as I stepped out into the crunchy snow. The fresh chill of the icy air sharp as a knife in my throat. I gasped, coughed.

We followed Dad, down the path winding around twisted metal, the vehicles' horrendous injuries softened by blankets of snow. 'Our' twisted hunk of snow-covered metal was situated at the front of the yard near an office. It had been placed there by smash repairs people so we could unload our things before it was towed into the depths of the car graveyard.

"Come on then," Dad said.

"We need to take out all the salvageable items and transfer them to the rental van. If you'd like to do that, while you're doing it, I will speak to the people in the office." Alright Dad I thought. We set to, forming a human chain, Lily inside the van or as far as possible as it was to get in, passing out pillows, quilts, books, cans of food, clothes, and every now and then, smashed remnants of Easter egg to which clung bright pink, sky blue, livid yellow, garish green, deep purple, or blood red foil.

Margy was first in line, then me, then Alex. We took turns in carrying items to the rental van, a preening mega-star with nary a scratch, and the merest smidgeon of today's light snow besmirching its immaculate roof. We were nearing the end of the task. Dad was in the wrecker's yard office talking to the people in charge. Lily had been in the van for some time, gathering last possessions. I was waiting for Margarita to pass the next things. In my pocket my fingers felt the sharp pieces of broken chocolate Easter egg that Dad had handed to me.

Not wanting to eat it, I had hidden it in my jacket pocket.

Now, absently my fingers ran over the foil covered shards. Lost in non-thought, I lifted a broken piece from my pocket. I peeled back foil and took a bite. I munched on it mechanically not even aware of what I was doing.

The drive back to the youth hostel through the white forest was relentlessly quiet.

Snow fell; the cold and silence of its pressure was increasing. I thought of the weightlessness of a snowflake, and the number of flakes that make up the weight of a snowdrift which materializes overnight, from nowhere, in a once familiar front garden.

And everything you thought you knew has disappeared.

Obscured by Nothing-ness. Whirling in a void.

We got out of the van and helped mum and dad pack up. I was the only one who had sustained a visible injury. No one took me to have a medical check-up. It didn't occur to anyone that I might be injured, that I might have concussion. That, if I'd hit my eye, I must have hit my head, and that, as I did not have a seatbelt on, my head must have slammed onto the dashboard, or steering wheel, or windscreen, or ceiling, as the van crashed. I must have seemed to be alright.

In my family, I was discovering, not mentioning something like that was considered the best policy, as if drawing attention to it would only make things worse for the wounded. At least that is why, I assumed, no-one and not even Margy, made any reference to the fact I was walking around, very quietly and somewhat woozily, only able to see out of one eye, the other a livid shiner. In hindsight, maybe my appearance made them feel uncomfortable.

We climbed into the new, new, van into which we'd heaped our possessions in jumbled piles. It seemed there was no point in trying to create a semblance of organisation or permanence. We were only going to be travelling in this hired van for the duration of our stay in Stockholm. All that mattered was that we get there. We would transfer our belongings into bags and continue our Easter journey by train without Dad. That was if all went to this new plan.

It snowed all the way to Stockholm but the postcard views and vistas of Sweden's capital, which at some previous time would no doubt have appeared jovial, Christmassy, somehow failed to charm as we made our way through the snow, along streets, to the harbour and the moored *Af Astrid*. I shivered thinking about sleeping on the yacht on the frozen water, like the lake we'd driven past on our way up the country. That we had so nearly crashed into.

"Please can we stay somewhere else, on land," I asked Mum. "It's reminding me of the lake where we crashed."

Mum said: "No. This is where we are staying."

I was anxious, numb. How could I sleep on the surface of this frozen lake? I was cold, in a daze.

It seemed utterly bizarre to me.

On the night of Easter, after we'd crashed next to a frozen lake, we had to sleep on the ice of a frozen lake. Inches beneath us was dark freezing water. Our mystery and miracle: we were all still alive.

Although it would take me a while to feel alive again.

24

WHITE WEEK
THE OCTAVE OF EASTER 1975

The days passed in a blur of white streets, cold feet as I miserably, dutifully, traipsed around various notable sights, museums and galleries of Stockholm. Due to my state, none of which impressed itself upon my memory. Nothing I saw or did made an impression on me. I felt too numbed and dazed to be able to realise it then. The nights were of fitful cold sleep of no rest for me on the frozen lake. One afternoon, we visited at her home, a colleague of Dad's, a capable blonde woman at the conference he was attending.

As soon as she saw me with my black eye, she gasped.

"Is she alright? Have you taken her to a hospital, do you need to?" She was not bothering with social niceties and cover ups, her concern for me was genuine and real. She was the first (and only) person who acknowledged to me or even 'saw' my black eye.

"She's alright," said Mum and Dad quickly. Although no medical person had looked at my injury. Neither of my parents had even mentioned it to me, or asked how I felt.

Dad's colleague did not seem convinced. She seemed more concerned about me than my parents, I thought. I felt uncomfortable at being the focus of this attention. We met her tall blonde daughter, and her daughter's tall blonde boyfriend.

Lily, Margy and I were entrusted to the care of her daughter and her boyfriend, as darkness and white snow fell, the young couple drove us to a cabin in a conifer forest by a frozen lake (was it the same one we had crashed next to or another, I had no idea).

The girl said it was their holiday home. Our hosts prepared thick hunks of bread and butter, which they passed around. They talked about Swedish comics and showed us one. It had cartoon images of exaggerated bodies in sexual acts which they laughed at uproariously. We didn't say anything.

The boyfriend played Bob Dylan songs on his guitar, and they all sang. Margy and Lily sang too. I was too dazed to sing, let alone laugh at or comment on images I found gross (and quite shocking), it was obviously a different culture in Sweden and they were older than us. Still I remember all this, whereas I do not recall any of the sights we went to in Stockholm, or what we did, all of which is lost in a fog of what was obviously my concussion.

They drove us back to the city through falling snow.

"Please could you slow down," I implored. I was so scared. The young man reduced speed. They could see my black eye; what no one could see was the terror I felt.

On Friday, Dad left on a plane for conferences elsewhere. Under the direction of Mum, with a collection of plastic bags filled with remnants of our luggage, we boarded a train which would carry us southwards. Sweden, Denmark, Germany, the Netherlands, Belgium to France.

The trip was unremarkable to me like everything. Stations, cities, towns, countries passed, the journey was punctuated by ticket collectors who slid open the door to our compartment, looked at our tickets, uttered words I could not understand, slid closed the door. Mercifully, when we reached our stop at a country station, and disembarked, the weather was warm and spring-like. Dad was on the platform to meet us; he escorted us out of the station to–another cream coloured rental van.

25

SECOND SATURDAY OF EASTER 1975

The youth hostel was in farmland. The days were blessed with golden sunshine. Clouds scudded breezily through the clear blue sky. The others set off on a long walk to a village. Except Dad. He was at another conference. They all seemed to be in high spirits. I still had a headache, a persistent ache accompanied by an overpowering feeling of faintness. Instead of going with them, I spent an afternoon in bed in the dormitory. My enclosure felt a little illicit, like lying in the sick bay at school. It felt as if I had suddenly, unexpectedly, escaped the rigours of normal capable routine existence, the disciplined exigencies of exertion exacted by health, and the energetic obligations which went with it.

Gratefully I lay on my back on the youth hostel bed; neck and head on a pillow. I felt as if my materiality had somehow lessened, as if the particles supposed to hold me together had moved further apart and I was suspended, hovering as faintly humming, golden, mote-filled sunbeams filled with whirling particles settled languorously in my supine unresisting form.

The remainder of the return voyage was uneventful. That was how the eldest girl experienced it, through a faint, misty sensation of feeling not-quite-right, ethereal and insubstantial. Margy and Lily roared with laughter at their own jokes and spoke to each other in a variety of mocking tongues. All I felt like doing was reclining, languid and detached, on a *chaise longue*, my hair loose on the pillow, quietly reciting fragmented lines of poems penned to tragic, doomed, youth... After two days and nights at the youth hostel, we drove to the port of Cherbourg and boarded the car ferry to Ireland.

The overnight ferry carried us to Rosslare; we arrived in the early morning. I perceived, and remember, it as a blur, we drove north, crossed the border, and on we went.

Spring had preceded us to County Antrim. Larger lambs grazed with their mothers in the fields; the hedgerows in the lanes that carried us homewards were sporting exuberant soft growth. An exhilarating hint of purple tinted the rhododendron bushes which flanked the drive; daffodils and primroses bloomed in a flower bed near the side of the house.

We had made it home. I experienced a sense of desolation. No-one said it, but surely we were all secretly reeling beneath the thought: what a holiday that was, not exactly one for the tourist brochures.

Dad pulled up outside the house in the new, new, new van, our fourth vehicle in a two-week trip. As it was only months before our move to Australia, departure date as yet undecided, dad said there was no point in buying a new van and we would keep on renting this van until we left. All being well, I thought grimly.

26
DAZED AND CONCUSSED
PASCHALTIDE 1975

The holiday in hell was over. The next day the big kids and the little kid donned school uniforms, picked up their school bags and headed to the halls of learning. Mum and Dad had deemed me well enough to go back to school. The afternoon before, Margy had been collected by her father who hurriedly exchanged Dusty and Jester for his daughter and whisked her back home.

I met her in the girls' cloakrooms, taking books out of her overhead locker. She turned her head and smiled at me with a rueful, conspiratorial expression, as if we were comrades who shared a secret.

"How are you? After fainting yesterday?" she asked.

"Okay. I had something to eat." I'd passed out briefly after walking into the house through the front door.

"Back to it." I murmured.

Margy twisted her lips cynically in assent.

"Come on!"

We were both a few minutes late, each having been dropped off late by our respective dads. We hurried. My platform soles sticking to the floor, towards the assembly-detention room.

No one mentioned my black eye to me, it was impossible not to notice, flamboyantly displaying a rainbow of mauves, purple, blue, green, yellow and red. (How did people think I got it? I wonder. But people must have just been being polite).

That morning, we had Art, my favourite subject. Last term I had decided I would illustrate a concept that had fascinated me: "Journey of the Soul."

In one work, I had painted a green hill, arching across the paper like the curve of the world. Above the green hill was blue sky. A black stick figure was running up the hill, over the curve.

Neither discernibly male nor female the figure's hair stuck out around a blankly generic non-face. The stick person held a bunch of balloon-heads on strings. Each balloon-head was a surreal face, in one drawing a couple of balloon heads were at loggerheads. In another, several balloon-heads detached from the stick-figure's hand and were flying away towards a moon in the sky composed of the ghostly white heads. I had drawn a series of sketches and chosen one to paint as my main work.

I entitled the work Conflict. When I showed my work to the class, Chester, an English boy I secretly admired said, to my surprise: "That's very good." He articulated his detailed response to the class. I had been silently gratified that someone had understood what it was about, especially someone whose intelligence impressed me or more specifically and truthfully, that I slightly fancied him, and he had said those serious, constructive things about my work.

In the same drawer was my work on Persephone, I'd made a series of sketches of the paradoxical goddess.

My poem's title caught my eye; I picked it up and read a few lines of my notes.

Hades, Ruler of the Underworld, sooner or later he'll get me, he'll get us all…

Suddenly, not knowing what I was doing, I ran from the room.

I had to escape!... My heart was beating fast. I walked to the front office. "Please could I have two painkillers, I have a headache," I said to the woman sitting at the desk behind the counter. She wordlessly handed me the foil wrapped pills, it seemed to signal to me that I was beneath contempt. I'd never seen any other expression on her face when she looked at me. Now her face lurched and swam giddily before my eyes.

Maybe I was getting a migraine. I'd never had one; Margy had them and described them in lurid detail. Sick headaches, aural effects, distorted vision, sessions of violent throwing-up. Margy occasionally came down with a migraine when she was staying at my house, and had to go to bed and lie down, I had brought her a bowl to be sick in, and a damp flannel to put on her brow. Since the crash I had been getting severe headaches accompanied by a sense of detachment. I took the pills to the girls' toilets where I washed them down with tap water sloshed into my cupped hands. I leaned against the white enamel sink and stared at the tiles on the floor. I felt as if I was neither here nor there, in a kind of limbo. Things which had once mattered so much to me: getting to class on time, the necessity of being in class, no longer seemed at all important to me.

It was as if all the obligations of normality, the day-to-day routine, which had until recently kept me in my usual place in life, had somehow loosened. And I was suspended in existential limbo.

What had once seemed so certain and unquestionable, was revealed to be full of gaps. The fabric of life, seemingly so substantial, appeared illusory. Now I knew that Life was capable of being blown away at any given moment to reveal the void, the realm of death beyond reality, our knowing world.

When we were driving through France to the ferry in the second rental van Dad had hired, we had seen a crashed lorry. The sight of it twisted on its side, filled me with an unbearable feeling of empathy.

"I hope the driver is all right," I said. Dad "tsk"-ed. Mum tut-tutted. My parents seemed irritated. My reaction was not considered acceptable, I realised, and that was another shock. As it had shocked me that Pa's death had not been mentioned by Dad or Mum after the announcement on the ferry. And it deeply shocked me that Dad drove us as he did in the blizzard. We were so nearly killed. I wondered if the driver of the lorry had died. "How could the driver survive that?" I'd asked in the van as we drove on. No one replied to my question.

Once, nothing made me cry. I had never seriously thought about or been aware of the difference between life and death, the divide like a string separating everything from nothing. Now I knew that there was nothing more precious than life, which you could lose instantly, at any moment.

"There you are–are you alright?" Margy came bustling into the girls' toilets. "I said I felt sick so I could find you and see what's happening. You're in big trouble for mooching out of class."

I scarcely bothered to shrug.

With the spectre of Death staring me down, the shocking knowledge that Death was all around, in front of me, all the time, just waiting, intertwined, reverberating through every stunned cell of my being, my getting into trouble for walking out of class seemed like a concern from another world.

I should have been resting at home. But that did not occur to anyone. Maybe if I had rested at home for longer, and ate, what happened to me next would not have.

27

IN LIMBO
THIRD SUNDAY OF PASCHALTIDE 1975

Sunday evening. Three weeks after the family, Margy and I returned from the holiday in hell. It'd been a warm spring day. It was all happening outside. Across the blue sky gusty breezes chased the clouds, lambs skipped and scampered in meadows, birds twittered in hedgerows and beech trees, spring growth cast a dreaming net of soft green leaves as the murder of crows cawed around the trees' high branches, behind the house.

I, Margy, and Lily had gone for a walk that took all day. An adventure. "Let's start walking and just keep walking and see where we end up!" Margy said. And, laughing at the absurdity and novelty of it, we did that. We set off in the mid-morning, with faithful Dusty bounding along beside us. We headed across a field, towards the mountain, knowing not where we were going, but going anyway.

We walked across fields, edges deep in dock leaves, nettles and thistles, or bright with yellow buttercup flowers, sticking to the hedgerows and fences, we headed in a wavering line away from the house. We hurried when we were walking through a cow pasture and a bull noticed us, and we had to jump over a water filled ditch. After a couple of miles we skirted a village and walked onwards. I was used to riding through the countryside. I had ridden in this direction along the narrow lanes. I'd never walked this way through the fields.

I hadn't eaten any breakfast that morning. The day before, I had eaten most of a packet of digestive biscuits with butter and a small tub of ice cream. When I woke up that morning I was sure the calories had converted to fat, metamorphosing into rolls of flab between my fingers. So I had decided to fast, to repent for my gastronomic sins, and attempt to achieve a perfect figure. Walking was good for that I believed.

When the three of us, Margy, Lily and I, arrived home we were tired and hungry.

"I'm starving," said Margy. "Lets make toasted sandwiches." Margy and Lily smothered slices of bread with butter, cheese and slices of tomato; snapping them together in the jaffle iron.

But I was determined to stick with my diet. I had a strong will and didn't find it difficult to ignore the grumbling hunger pains. Au contraire. On the contrary. I was pleased my stomach was rumbling. That meant it wasn't full of food.

After their toasted sandwiches, Margy and Lily ate dinner with the family, spaghetti followed by fruit. I ate nothing.

Instead of eating, I went to my room. I read my book of Japanese poetry on my bed, listening to music.

As sometimes happened, Margy and I were going to sleep on a mattress on the floor in Lily's room. Lily sometimes was frightened of The Ghost. She didn't want to be alone and asked me to sleep in her room. Or she would try to creep into my bed in the middle of the night saying how scared she was. Lily would wake me up, knocking on my door, calling my name. Sometimes she came and shook me awake. She would stand at my bedroom door, whimpering: "Please can I sleep with you, I'm scared. Please, please let me sleep with you. Go on, please, please. Oh, go on, go on. I'm really scared of the ghost."

Until I relented or else shouted at her to shut up and go away and let me get back to sleep. Though I didn't feel good about it later when I was fully awake in the light of day, and remembered the night before. It made me feel awful to realise I had been so mean to my little sister.

Then a few months earlier Lily had dragged a spare mattress up to her room and left it on the floor next to the radiator on her wall. When Margy wasn't staying, and when she was, I slept on the mattress on Lily's floor.

On this particular evening, Margy and I were both sleeping together on the single mattress on the floor in Lily's room. It was about ten pm. Light filtered in from the hallway downstairs through the half-opened door. Margy lay beside me, on one side, facing the wall. I lay on my back. I was drifting in a relaxed pre-sleep state, not thinking of anything. Thinking of... nothing.

Now, my fingers ran over the foil covered fragments. Lost in non-thought, I lifted a handful of cold broken pieces from my pocket. I peeled back the foil and took a bite. I munched on it mechanically not even aware of what I was doing.

My heart beat wildly.

Opening before me like an infinitely immense chasm, the chasm of death I was about to enter, hurtling at the speed of light, terror, into that chasm, that never-ending darkness, into the unknown...

I was dying!

I sat upright, gasping, struggling for breath. My hand flew to my throat, as if to check my pulse.

"What's wrong?" Margy woke and sat up; her face creased with concern.

Lily woke and sat upright in her bed. "What is it?"

The air in the bedroom crackled with panic.

"Get Dad," I gasped.

Margy and Lily jumped up and ran from the room, calling "Marcus! Marcus! Dad!"

Dad was in the TV room watching the news.

He walked in with them, his gait relaxed and calm.

"What's up?" he asked reassuringly, crouching down next to the mattress. I sat up, almost passing out.

"I don't know," I gasped, tumbling, backwards, fast, down a bottomless well.

"I think I'm dying!"

"No, you're not dying," Dad said calmly. "What did you eat today?"

"Nothing," I gasped.

"Ah, that's what it is then!" he said. "You need something to eat. You can't go for a day without eating anything! What would you like?"

"Oatmeal biscuits," I said weakly, falling through space. I could feel and hear each of my heartbeats as it thundered and crashed through my body. I was sure each one was the last. I was dying.

Food, if only food could help me I would eat a bathtub full of food.

"Girls would you please go down to the kitchen and get some food for Roxy. Lily your mother is there." Dad requested. His calm presence was reassuring, but it didn't stop me falling, hurtling towards my death.

Margy and Lily hurried off together, whispering in concern. I could hear their footsteps, disappearing down the stairs. They returned, an infinity later, carrying trays piled high with food.

Lily passed me a plate of oatmeal biscuits; she had baked them herself yesterday. I picked one up and took a bite.

My mouth filled with crumbs.

I felt as if I was choking as the food passed into my throat.

Out of control, zigzagging, a blizzard in front of me.

"Keep eating," Lily urged.

"Yes, come on, eat as much as you can," Margy said.

"Eat up," said Dad.

Dutifully, doing my best to please them, I kept on eating. I ate the biscuits. I ate a slice of buttered banana bread, made yesterday by Lily. I sipped the tea which Margy handed to me.

"There now, she's got her colour back," Margy said.

"You look a lot better," Dad said. "You must eat."

"I've had enough, thank you," I lay my head on the pillow.

"Okay girls, time for lights out," said Dad. "I'll see you in the morning."

"Goodnight Dad," said Lily.

"Goodnight Marcus," said Margy.

"Night, Dad," I said faintly.

I could feel each heartbeat reverberating through my body, crashing through every cell and atom of consciousness. Each heartbeat like the moment I knew the van was about to crash. It felt like a repetition, that each heartbeat was going to be my last. (And it literally was. The last heartbeat, before the next). I was panicking.

Nothing made any sense.

I couldn't sleep for hours, then I fell into a restless stupor, and had a nightmare that was so real I felt I was awake:

I was alone in the house. There was something in the house, a force, a presence, approaching. The Ghost! I was alone in the house with the Ghost!

A feeling of absolute terror pervaded every cell and fibre of my being.

I was dying.

I opened my eyes, gasping, panicking; struggling for breath.

The room was bathed in darkness. On the bed beneath the window, Lily's body lay. I could see the rising and falling of my sister's breathing beneath the duvet.

Next to me, Margy slept. I could hear and see her breathing, as she inhaled and exhaled rhythmically, automatically.

I was fighting for my breath; I was spinning out in terror. I was about to die! Again and again with each heart beat I faced death. It was happening again. I was about to die.

The night passed in waking and sleeping nightmares. The next morning I couldn't wake properly. I was not-there. I was in the nightmare zone. I got up and went through the actions of my normal routine: ablutions in the bathroom, dressing in my uniform, eating breakfast and collecting things for school.

I went into the stable yard and replenished the water in the ponies' buckets; gave them some hay.

Back in the house everyone was getting ready, Margy, Lily, Alex, Sarah and Dad rushing around, gathering everything needed for their day away from the house. Mum stood in the kitchen in her dressing gown, her hair hanging in wavy locks around her face.

I climbed awkwardly into the van. Me, Margy, Alex, and Sarah, all squashed up together on the back seat like sardines in a can. Lily in the front; she and Alex were dropped off at the bus stop. But the "normality" of the start to the day, squashed up on the van seat with Margy and my siblings didn't stop me from being aware of every one of my heartbeats, didn't stop me from being convinced each beat of my heart was going to be the last.

This is it–I'm about to die. Nothing could stop me from hurtling towards my death now–

...absently my fingers ran over the foil covered shards. Lost in non-thought, I lifted a handful of broken pieces from my pocket. I peeled back the foil and took a bite. I munched on it mechanically not even aware of what I was doing–

not even aware of what–

I spent my day unable to concentrate or focus on anything apart from my panicked fear.

"It's like when we were in the van, when I realised we were about to crash," I said to Mum urgently in the kitchen when we got home. I was trying to communicate to her what I was going through.

"It's the same feeling I had when I knew that Dad had lost control of the van. It's the feeling of knowing I'm going to die.

I can feel every one of my heartbeats, and I think each one is going to be the last, I keep thinking I'm about to die!"

Mum didn't say anything.

There was a look of disapproval on her face as she plunged her arm into the paper sack and, with her bare hand, pulled out a poor dead cow's heart and slapped it down on the cutting board. Dusty waited expectantly. I turned and climbed the stairs back to my room and then climbed into my bed.

I took the next few days off school but that did not make anything, or nothing, better. It did not make Nothing better. That did not make sense. Lying in bed or wandering the house were terrifying. At night I couldn't sleep. If I did manage to slip into restive slumber, I had hideous nightmares, about the ghost. I was alone in the house with the ghost; and the ghost was out to get me.

The feeling of unbearable terror woke me again and again—into a waking nightmare. Fingertips pressed in terror to my pulse, on my slim wrists or my throat, I felt each throb of my life blood pulse, convinced it was the last.

The only time I had any brief relief from this horror was when I was eating. As I ate, I forgot my heartbeat. I felt like I used to when I ate, which was not aware of myself, I was just aware of the sensation of eating, the delicious taste of the food and the sensation of it filling my mouth and sliding down my throat as I swallowed. As soon as I stopped eating panic set in again. I went for walks by myself to try to escape it.

I walked from the house, down the hill to the river. Then I walked along the grassy riverbank until I reached the stone bridge where the lane crossed the river. I climbed up a steep earthen track to the narrow lane, and I stood on the bridge, arms leaning on lichened stone. I stared downwards into the clear ripples of the shallow water gurgling around grey rocks and stones. But it didn't make me feel better.

I was hyper-aware of every one of my heartbeats. With each one, my panic concentrated at the fever pitch of terror. With each heartbeat I was about to die. *This is it*. Again. And again.

...Lost in non-thought, I lifted a handful of broken pieces from my pocket. I peeled back the foil and took a bite. I munched on it mechanically not aware of what I was doing.

With my head turned to the grey pebbled surface of the lane, I walked up the small hill from the river bend, back to the house. Birds twittered; lambs skipped. On either side of the lane, verges were deep in green grass, studded with wildflowers. Hedgerows fragrant with blossom. Yellow primroses. I was cut off from it, as if I was in another in-between dimension, I walked through the driveway entrance, flanked by tall stone pillars, entwined with ivy. The wrought iron gates were open. I walked up the drive planted with rhododendrons the height of trees, bursting into a riotous frenzy of bright purple blossoms.

Phoenix, Crackers, and Berry were all out, pastured in the front field, on the far side of the rhododendron hedge. They could not see me but must have been aware of me as I walked up the drive.

When I reached the wooden gate at the top of the field in a gap in the hedge they were all waiting, gently snorting and pawing the ground, eager for their evening meal.

"Hey, Phoenix. Waiting for your hay, hey hey?"

I blew down his nostrils, the way horses greet each other. But none of the things I did, made me feel grounded, nothing made me feel like myself, it was as if I was out of my body and my mind was struggling to get back in. What was going on?

Now, absently my fingers ran over the foil-covered shards. Lost in non-thought, I lifted a handful of broken pieces from my pocket. I peeled back the foil and took a bite. I munched on it mechanically not even aware of what I was doing.

"It's the same. I can feel every one of my heartbeats and I keep thinking each one is going to be the last." I said to Mum, in the kitchen. I pleaded. "Please, I have to see a doctor."

"We need an appointment to see the doctor," Mum said evenly. "I can't just take you there. The medical centre is closed now, anyway. It's after five o'clock."

I could hear my voice rising. "I can feel every heartbeat in my body and I know each one is going to be the last! You've got to take me to the doctor!"

My mother sighed. "I'll make an appointment for you to see Severin Lyons tomorrow," she said.

Then she got on with making supper.

After another night of hell I woke at seven am. "I can't go to school," I said. "There's something wrong with my heart."

That afternoon, Mum drove me to the clinic in town to see our family doctor.

"Hello Isobel," he said, at the door of his consulting room; ushering us in, with a professional smile.

"Hello Severin," Mum said in the confidential 'grown up' tone she used in speaking to her trusted peers.

"Take a seat." He gestured.

We all sat down. The doctor at his consulting desk. Mum in the chair opposite him. Me next to mum.

There was a moment of expectant silence.

"Well," he said. "And what brings us here today?"

The last time I had seen Doctor Lyons had been in the first year we were living here. It was before I met Margy, before I had been put down a year. Not long after we moved into The Old Manse and I had come down with the strange, lingering, indefinable low-grade viral illness.

Since then, if I felt ill it was when Margy was staying, and we would spend the day off school, reading, making trips to the kitchen when Mum went to collect Sarah from school; we'd stock up on platefuls of food which we carried up to my room on trays. That was in the world before the crash.

Mum and the doctor turned their eyes expectantly to me.

"It's my heart," I said. "There's something wrong with my heart."

My mother sighed in scarcely concealed exasperation.

"In what way do you think there is something wrong with your heart," said Doctor Lyons in a kindly tone.

"I can feel every heartbeat in my body, and I think each one is going to be the last, I keep thinking I am about to die."

"Hmm," he said looking at me inscrutably. "How old are you now?"

"Fifteen. Almost sixteen," I replied.

"And how is everything in the rest of your life—have you been having problems with anything? Is anything troubling you?"

"Everything's fine, Severin," said my mother. "She doesn't have any problems."

"What would you say?" He looked at me encouragingly.

"Well," I said slowly. "We're moving to Australia this year. I've been worried about that. And we were in a bad van crash."

"Oh," said Mum in a reassuring tone. "We had a family car accident on holiday in Europe, at Easter, Severin, but nobody was hurt."

"I got a black eye," I muttered.

"No one was *seriously* hurt," Mum said.

He picked up my wrist and pressed two finger pads against its underside, holding his fingers there for a minute.

"You have a good strong pulse," he said.

"Are you sure?" I said doubtfully.

"Yes, you do, it feels fine."

"This is what we'll do," he continued in a calm tone.

"We have a machine for testing people's hearts. We use it to test a range of patients for all sorts of heart problems. If there are any irregularities in your heart, the machine will detect them. What we need is you to be hooked up to the machine for a few minutes. That way we get an accurate reading."

"Oh Severin, we don't want to put you to so much trouble! Isn't that for people who are seriously ill?" Mum said, sounding a bit alarmed.

"I'll just go and tell the nurse to prepare it," said the doctor, standing up.

Mum did not say anything while he was away.

He returned, and said briskly: "Come this way." I followed him into a room where the electrocardiograph machine was situated. He attached metal plates with wires onto my wrists, and I was left alone in the room.

When the doctor returned a few minutes later, he scanned the results quickly.

"You have a good strong heart. There's nothing wrong with it at all."

"Are you sure there's nothing wrong with my heart?"

"No there's nothing wrong," he smiled kindly and carefully at a spot behind my left shoulder.

Back in his consulting room, he told my mother the same thing. "That should be all that's needed now," he said as if in code. "But come back and see me if things don't settle down."

He smiled again, and escorted us to the door.

"Goodbye Roxanne. Goodbye Isobel."

"Goodbye Severin," said Mum.

"Bye," I said.

Mum did not say anything on the drive home. I imagined I could feel disapproval emanating from her like some kind of scary perfume. I didn't know why she should be so put out. After all, Mum wasn't the one teetering on the brink of an internal abyss. I didn't believe there was nothing wrong. He must have made a mistake. Could the machine have been malfunctioning? I didn't feel better. I felt the same hyper-awareness of each heartbeat, convinced each would be the last, and I was terrified.

That night I was too scared to go to sleep because I had the nightmare of the ghost when I drifted off. When I woke it was worse, in the shadows of my room, the habitat of the ghost, I was immobilised inside my nightmare.

Was I awake or asleep? I was too scared to move let alone jump out of bed and run to Lily's room.

Somehow time passed and I battled to overcome the frozen lock, the stranglehold, of fear. Somehow I managed to stumble upwards from my bed, stagger into Lily's room and into her bed beside her. Everything was topsy-turvy and upside down. Whereas before it had been Lily begging me for shelter from fear at night in the creepy house, now it was me who was desperately trying to escape terror. What was going on?

Two days later, my mother took me back to our doctor.

"I don't feel any different," I said. "I can feel every heartbeat in my body and I keep thinking that each one is the last. I keep thinking that I am just about to die. There must be something wrong with my heart. Please can I go on that machine again, so you can find out."

It was hard to explain and describe then what I was feeling, it seemed illogical. Although I think it was psychologically logical: I had faced death and so now I had a close consciousness of death, brought on by the physical trauma of the crash and the physiological trauma that it had caused in me, and my body and mind had articulated it in a metaphor, however, could I also have arrhythmia, an irregular heartbeat, brought on by the physical trauma, which can be fatal, maybe I really was in danger of dying imminently. Was is possible that the machine would not have detected it in a few minutes? Maybe it would have needed much longer, or maybe it would never have picked it up. What I had was a form of 'post-traumatic stress disorder,' which in 1975 had not been given that name yet. I was doing my best to get help for myself. To stay alive. To save myself from Death. I wasn't mad. All these thoughts go through my mind now, many years later.

My mother and the doctor exchanged glances.

"Yes, you can, I'll go and ask the nurse to get it ready," he said, standing up.

After I had the second test, when I returned to his room, and sat beside Mum, the doctor said carefully, "There's nothing wrong with you physically," his words were slow, precise and calm. He paused. "What you have is an anxiety neurosis."

"What's that?" I asked.

"Psychological symptoms caused by anxiety," he replied. "There is neurosis then psychosis. This is not a psychosis," he said, smiling in a professional manner. Mum's expression had switched from long-suffering to icy. I wonder could she have been frozen in anxiety too? Was it really only me?

"Does she have a boyfriend?" he asked brightly, looking at Mum.

My mother looked disapproving and did not deign to reply.

"Well now," the doctor continued in his bedside manner, as if he hadn't noticed he had just dropped a social bomb.

"I'm going to prescribe Serendium, one tablet to be taken three times a day. To be continued as long as necessary. That should help matters. If there are any further problems, come and see me."

He finished writing the script then stood up, handing it to Mum. "You can get the prescription filled out at the pharmacy in the clinic. Best to start straight away."

"Thank you, Severin," said Mum in what I recognised as an arctic tone, as his smile broadened. Or maybe my memory exaggerates.

"Goodbye Roxanne. Goodbye Isobel!"

"Goodbye," we said.

I took the first pill in the kitchen when we returned home from the medical centre. I washed it down with a tumbler of water and then went up to my room.

On a wall in my room was a poster of Proserpine, by one of the artists in the movement which Margy, Lily and I admired. We had bought discounted posters in a record shop in town. Persephone, Queen of the Underworld, the goddess of fertility and spring growth and death in Ancient Greek mythology. In Roman mythology, the 'same' goddess was called Proserpine.

I lay on my bed and gazed at the image of the green robed figure. Goddess of Fertility and Queen of the Underworld. Of new life, rebirth and of the underworld of the dead. It seemed to be a paradoxical combination, in a world where everything seemed to have to be one thing or the other. Catholic/Protestant, dutiful daughter or girlfriend, sick/well, alive or dead…

Persephone's hair, darker than mine, was swept high above her brow. Her dark eyes burned mysteriously. One long-fingered white hand grasped her wrist as if she was checking her pulse. The other held the pomegranate, split open, revealing a row of seeds from which, in a state of mythical forgetfulness, she had eaten–three in some accounts, more in others.

In Hades, in the shadows and depths of the underworld, Persephone herself forgot. She ate the pomegranate seeds, like swallowing a medicinal pill, one for each meal of the day.

The unbearable tension which had increased until I was at breaking point eased, a great soft calmness slowly washed into me, taking the edges off the afternoon. I felt my limbs loosen and relax. My head sank gratefully onto the pillow, my anxiety abated, *nothing matters anymore, nothing matters…* the words sounded through my imagination, as if spoken by the goddess herself.

It's okay now, you can relax, forget everything, just relax, relax and let yourself go.

The Serendium softened the edges of my terror. After I took the first tranquilizer I could sleep without being woken by nightmares. I developed a laid back, worldly detachment. In the daytime when my siblings were out at school, I lay on my bed, listening to records on the record player. As I listened to an album Dora had lent me and Lily, my lips formed a smile of faint detachment.

Nothing seemed to matter anymore. Whereas previously I had spent much of my time at grammar school in one form of trouble or another, it wasn't because I didn't care about school, or anything. It was more that I cared too much; an endeavour doomed to failure.

But now, I really didn't care about anything. When I went to school, which was not often now (what was the point I was moving to Australia) I wandered along the school corridors in a muzzy daze. All the edges had been smoothed off everything so that it felt as if I was cocooned in thick, all-absorbent cotton wool. I was aware of my heart beating, sometimes this almost became acute, but it didn't worry me as it had. Or, at least, I couldn't feel it so much. Before taking the Serendium, all my feelings, emotions, and sense of self, of 'me,' had been locked together in a natural, but almost fatal, embrace. Now that fear and my Self had become detached from each other, the fear still existed but it did not get through to me, in the way it had before. The problem for me was nothing got through to me, my emotions and moral sense were blunted. Submerged. I felt a bit better than I had, but I was still not cured.

"I don't feel so scared about my heart stopping anymore," I said to Margy one day. "But I don't feel anything else either!" I didn't feel surprise, or shock or happiness. Even the prospect of my family's impending move to Australia had lost its terrifying end-of-the-universe-as-we-know-it aspect. Inner terror wrapped in cotton wool.

PART TWO

AGNES AND THE STIRLINGTONS

The Manse.
County Antrim, Ireland
1848-1860

28

THE MANSE

February 1860

"I see there's an article in the paper about that book on evolution." Reverend Austin Stirlington peered over his pince-nez, above his weekly newspaper the *Argus* (delivered only five days late). "And it's on the same page as an article on the attempt to corral all the words ever used in our language in a definitive English dictionary that is intended to record the evolution of meaning in English as a colonial language. Ha!"

His grey bushy eyebrows raised, eyes twinkling in a genial sardonic smile, he looked at his lady wife at the opposite end of the civilised expanse of the breakfast table.

Mrs Victoria Stirlington stopped eating her porridge.

She regarded her husband, sitting opposite her in his black coat, black cassock and white clerical collar. A ray of sunshine slanted through a gap in the lace curtains behind him, illuminating his grey hair and the grey whiskers framing his face.

"Indeed?" she said, a grimace of disapproval tightening her lips.

"It's caused the social equivalent of an earthquake since it was published in November 1859. Interesting, is it not, that was the same year that the Ulster Revival in religious conversions began not far from here in County Antrim. That is also having a seismic effect."

"Hmm," said his lady wife, in her non-committal way.

"This essayist is saying that the theory of evolution is not necessarily incompatible with the view of the world and living things being created by God, that is the line that he is arguing in the paper today."

"How is that so?" asked Mrs Stirlington.

"The argument goes that it is God's will that species evolve *biologically* as the *scientific* author says and that God is nonetheless still the prime creator."

Doctor Stirlington had been a medical doctor in County Down; it was his brother Cyril, who held the title of Viscount Stirlington, who had suggested he transform his life, in the days of the horror that was the Great Famine. The doctor had never imagined he would one day be meeting the demands of the Revival in Presbyterianism that surely no one could have anticipated would be extraordinarily transforming masses of people in a fervour of emotional 'conversions' to 'faith', to use the terms of the day that were quoted in newspapers and on people's lips around here.

Doctor Stirlington had deliberated Cyril's request that he take up a ministry of God, he'd been a well-liked physician and local figure in his practice, with a reputation for healing the body and psyches of his patients when he was working as a doctor before the Great Famine began in the mid-1840s when he had first seen the grotesque clay figurines his brother had brought back from his adventures of exploration in Africa and put them in his house. The manor was owned by Lord Cyril Stirlington, House of Lords peer, as part of his estate of lands in Counties Antrim, Fermanagh, and Cavan, that had been tenanted by 'tenants at will' and potato gardeners. Their crops had failed in the years of the Great Famine.

Along with all the tenants there, his brother's tenants, with no crops to sell, could not pay their rent–which was due twice a year every May the first and November the first. They were all evicted. They had no potatoes to eat, their staple crop. A million people had died from disease: fever, typhus, cholera, dysentery, which spread across much of Ireland. To save themselves, a million impoverished people of all ages emigrated to America, Canada, and Australia; many died on the voyage.

Cyril was a landowner who had realised it was cheaper to pay emigration fares for his starving tenants after they had become impoverished by the potato famine or Great Hunger, than to pay an annual tax for his impoverished pauper tenants to be housed in the workhouse or set to work on the Public Works roads projects. The roads to nowhere. At the start of the famine, the British government had authorised soup kitchens for the starving. But soon under *laissez faire* economic reforms, they changed their approach and made people work on the 'roads projects' twelve hours a day, from six am to six pm for a pittance to buy food, and if they were late to work their pay of pennies a day was reduced and if they arrived after ten am they were paid nothing. Starving people had to cut the solid rock the roads wound through, and they had to break up rock to make the roads. Unrecorded, forgotten to the archives, many many people died. They were buried in mass graves near the unfinished roads. (Not one of them was ever finished).

The Reverend Doctor remembered, pulling himself back to the present on his rare day of respite from his church work. Yet, then he drifted in reverie again, his thoughts continuing in their rather anxious journey back into the past, and all the difficult years that had led to here, on the road he had taken at a crossroads. Some troubling memories repeated in his mind, in fragments, that jumbled together.

29

A BRUTAL ROULETTE, 1848

Cyril had said to his doctor brother as he first showed him around the manor house: "Emigration has the advantage of ridding landlords' estates of 'pauperism,' clearing the land the landlords could use for more productive farming–of beef cattle and of grain for export to England and the territories of empire where British Army soldiers are stationed around the world, in Bombay, Calcutta, America, Australia and here too in Ireland. It is a global market. They need to eat..."

Cyril said his maid Breena's friend Nola was one of the girls whom he had personally recommended be selected and taken by horse drawn carriage to Dublin as part of the Earl 's scheme to help famine orphans.

"A selected group of girls of marriageable age has been taken from workhouses, and sailed to England to be sent from London to Melbourne in a fleet of sailing ships. She is on the first. Nola's intended destiny is to work as a domestic, marry, and bear children to help populate the colony in Australia."

Cyril explained to his brother that Breena was one of his tenants' daughters. "After both her parents and all her siblings died and to spare her the horrors of the workhouse, I brought her to work here in this house of mine in County Antrim. I am aware that the fates of the majority of those who emigrate may not be as rosy as I hope Breena's friend Nola turns out to be. I hear that emigrants are dying on the journey from Ireland, but I think it is best seen as a matter of economics. And evolution, my dear brother. 'Survival of the fittest'? Progress. I have heard some are expected to do well in the new world."

What an odious perspective, thought the Doctor.

"Yes." Cyril continued as he hastened to the second storey, up the staircase, with his brother following, and paused in the hall to summarise his economic theory.

"When there are a thousand paupers in the workhouse it is cheaper to offer free passage to America to all of them than to keep the pauperised tenants in the workhouse which in 1845 cost five thousand pounds per annum in overall social welfare tax calculated in the first year of the famine when the potato crops failed; it was projected it would be the same the next year and likely the year following that, this year, as seems to be proving to be the case."

Cyril said: "I worked out that at the end of the first year of the famine in 1845, if every man, woman and child in the workhouse, or working on the roads, accepted free passage to emigrate that it would not exceed five thousand pounds, as I said, bear with me, so it was cheaper to provide them with free passage than keep them in the workhouse and working on the roads-to-nowhere—and all the chaos of that, which has to be dealt with."

Doctor Stirlington had a compelling perspective for taking up the offer, he hoped it would save him from working with the dying, and catching a 'road fever' himself, what would his family do if that happened?

He said in a non sequitur: "I know of the fatal symptoms of 'road disease'—dysentery, typhus and cholera which afflict the people who work on the public works roads-to-nowhere scheme with its horrors (and those who are turned out onto the roads, their cabins burnt by landlords leaving them destitute). I have seen the dead bodies that people thought were alive as their muscles twitch and convulse, corpses that suddenly sit upright in coffins awaiting burial, leading to the stories of the living dead. Some sit up as recently dead muscles contract in spasms. A similar effect is the sound of knocking from inside a coffin when the corpse of a person who has died of the 'road diseases' is being buried. This has led to coffins being opened to reveal the corpse, who a doctor or priest must again testify is dead. The knocking is caused by reflex twitching of the limbs or the hands of a corpse hitting the coffin lid from inside. That is giving rise to the spate of horror stories in the newspapers. I read one in the *Argus* yesterday, did you see it, Cyril?"

It was a tangent but that was how he coped, he knew that. Maybe he was not meant to be a medical doctor after all. But it was human not to want to die and to prefer to read a horror story than to see the real thing and be exposed to catching the 'road disease'. (He was at heart a coward even when it came to blood, the sight of which could make him feel queasy, and he knew that about himself too).

"I have avoided 'road disease' by avoiding close contact with ill people," said the Doctor to his brother. "It is too dangerous to treat; doctors I knew who braved treating patients in work-houses have died a wretched death. Those road diseases, do not discriminate." He confided to Cyril about this as they stood together on a Persian rug in the hallway in front of a window that looked towards a mountain on the horizon. Both were so engrossed in their different preoccupations, that neither paid attention to the calming vista belying the havoc of famine. It all seemed to be going round in circles. Because of course it was still in the midst of the famine years then.

Cyril said: "The workhouse has been joined by the options of the Poor Laws offered by the government for tenant farmers and their families who are starving to death. Another option is Board of Works Public Works employment for the poor through the program of building roads, which may well start and end in a bog going nowhere, but the purpose is to pay the evicted workers a pittance, in the hope they can buy food, but there is no food for them to buy; all the edible food is being exported to England–wheat, beef, eggs–and the poor starving evictees are the ones who have to produce it, transport it and get it to market, loading it onto the ships with the last shreds of strength they have left. (For the condition of tenancies was that in return for a cabin and a patch of land to grow potatoes, they must pay rent and give service, working in the production and preparation of crops and eggs, and beef, for their landlord, and they could not eat that food. No. They had to do all the hard work of producing it, to make money for their landlord.) Then they will likely die. There is a program called "outdoor relief," soup kitchens outside, where food is handed to the starving people to complement what we call "indoor relief," the workhouse, under the Poor Laws. But not enough food reaches the people, they are given starvation rations, if they get any food, and tragically they are dying in the hundreds of thousands of road disease and famine fever."

"Aye. It is a brutal roulette, as to who lives, who dies, who reaches the lands they were dreaming of, and how they survive when they arrive, if they ever do," said the Doctor to himself.

"In effect," Sir Cyril said brutally, "the evictions are a mass clearance of my non-productive lands. It is a question of capitalistic economics, and modernisation."

That was the rationalization being used, as if it were a war. Some were calling the famine a "genocide," thought Austin as Cyril showed him the master bedroom and the study.

Cyril said it made more money to use his cleared land for grazing cattle. "There is a great hunger for beef in England.

And salted beef in British territories. Money to pay for it."

Doctor Stirlington had not laughed at his brother's words which were in appalling taste. What about the hunger of the people here for food? he thought. The starving former tenant farmers who produced the food, had to take it to the boats and load it on and watch it sail away. Leaving none for the starving here. All the families. Hundreds of thousands homeless, dead and dying. The Doctor thought it was unethical; he certainly knew it was, he had an inner moral compass, his own views, that he often kept to himself. And he did not say much about that now, on this day. Or ever.

"I will think about it, brother," was all he had said.

30
"TAKE MY HOUSE. BECOME A MINISTER OF GOD"
1851

The brutal colonialist Lord Stirlington had offered his brother the manor house and an acreage around it, when he evicted, broke up and dispersed the cabin or 'cottier' farmers' potato gardens and tumbled their cottages on his lands. Now the tenant families were gone, most of the men, women and children had died after they were evicted, their homes had been pulled down and burnt so they could never return.

"It is progress. Making money, by asserting control, is what it is all about," said Cyril to Doctor Stirlington as once again they walked around the upsettingly grand manor house, the two of them together.

"In Ulster, by imparting and upholding the values of being "saved" you, dear brother, can help to guide desperate people onto the right path, through preaching, to offer spiritual hope of being born again," said Cyril.

"The people need to unleash their deep misery; their pain; they need to have the hope of being saved. Saved from the horrors they witnessed and experienced: eviction, emigration, starvation, so many who died whose lives were not saved; who were starved, forced out, lives and families shattered. They do not understand why England has allowed the continued exports of the food they the tenant farmers produced for their landlords' estates in the famine. As Ireland exported the eggs, beef, and grain to England, and the British colonies, everywhere British soldiers are to feed them, Ireland's population, and the tenants producing the food, were not allowed to eat, becoming ill with famine fever, and starving to death. It could happen again; potato crops could fail again (although now we have evicted, broken up and destroyed the people's potato gardens and farms on our land). Here in Ulster, which is also dependent on the linen industry, the people are not destitute in quite the same numbers, some had work in the linen trade, and could buy food, and all were not wholly reliant on their potatoes. Yes, half the population of County Fermanagh died. Almost a third of the population of County Cavan, and of County Monaghan. Yes, there is the craving to be saved."

Really, his brother went too far with his oratory, once he got started, thought Doctor Stirlington when his brother had proposed it. Did he not care about what he was ranting about? But he was mild mannered (and had thought his family would benefit from a larger property) and all he said, amiably, was:

"As you put it so eloquently dear brother, how can I refuse?"

Before the Stirlington brothers left the house, Cyril had rung a bell in a front reception room as they stood by a central fireplace, and a curly-black-haired young maid in a long white pinafore apron over a beige linen dress opened the door, after knocking, and being ordered to enter by the viscount.

"Our coats please Breena," said Cyril.

"Yes, sir," she said bobbing in a small curtsey.

"Breena, this is my brother Doctor Stirlington, you may be seeing more of him and his family before long."

"Yes, sir." She bobbed again in the doctor's direction, then gracefully turned and left the room to fetch their overcoats.

As a condition of his brother Austin's accepting Cyril's offer of the house, and changing his vocation to minister, Cyril said that the servants would remain to look after the house, stables, horses, fields and gardens. That would include Breena. Cyril would, he said, take care of the servant's wages. As Cyril was the eldest he had inherited their father's estate, and his brother was indebted to him for his generosity, which included setting up a trust fund for his ministry and life here with his family.

Meanwhile, Cyril decamped to his Park Row mansion in London, and planned his next expedition abroad.

He was going back to Africa.

The family comprising Doctor Stirlington, Mrs Stirlington and their children whose number had grown to include Agnes (eight), Timothy (four), and Prudence (one), moved into the Manse as it was now called, after the doctor took on his role of church minister. Since then, after studying for months and preparing a stock of sermons, he had preached day and night at his church. He did not find it too onerous to preach to the people.

That was nine years ago.

31

SAVED. TO BE BORN AGAIN, 1860

It was now years since the start of the Great Hunger, when many of the population of Ireland tragically died of starvation, or emigrated to try to save themselves, and now there seemed to be no limit to the demand of people to be converted, to be "born again," to atone, to be saved, and the "salvation" services held inside, and outside, the church were emotional, and driven by fear; Reverend Stirlington had witnessed countless numbers of people make confessions of their "sins" with a fervour that was extraordinary, awe-inducing to behold, they entered trances, sobbed, they pleaded forgiveness for penances, they begged to be saved; it gave them comfort. Conversions were followed by the next new wave seeking to be reborn, and so it continued. Day after day. Some thought it miraculous. Other commentators were sceptical, and cynical.

It would later be said that a hundred thousand people had converted to evangelical Presbyterianism during these intense years of the 'Ulster Revival' as it was being termed. Every day of every week, the Reverend Stirlington set off with his groom in his horse-drawn carriage to post to his church. He had to tend his flock. For the last few days, though, he had stayed here. His powers of healing were needed here in his own house.

Agnes had been watching him speak as he weighed up the merits of creationism and scientific theory. She supposed that as a medical man, a doctor, he was a man of science. And if the truth be known, he was interested, in many ways, in these new ideas, but he would keep his enthusiasm to himself, at home. It was advisable to be circumspect, he believed.

His daughter did not know how it was that he could separate

his mind that was interested in these new ideas and theories, from feelings aroused by the dire state of the household. But her father seemed to be relishing his time away from church work, to be able to talk about other things, and relax without posting off to church, as he did every day with their groom in their horse-drawn carriage, to convert and preach to the men, women and children, until late, when Arthur the groom drove him home in the carriage.

"What do you think, Agnes?" her father looked at her, with a smile. "Do you think that creationism and evolutionism are compatible according to God's design of the world, or is the theory a heresy?" He had more engaging discussions with his daughter than his wife; he was interested to hear her view.

But today she could not hold back her emotion.

"Father, I cannot think about such things," she exclaimed. "When Timmy is lying upstairs, unconscious in his bed. You are supposed to be here to cure him."

"I know, my dear," he replied mildly. "And as you are aware that is what I am endeavouring to do. I have given Timmy the medicine I sent away for which arrived yesterday, and we can pray with God's grace, that he will be better soon." He smiled at his eldest daughter again, encouragingly.

"Well, I can't think about anything else," said Agnes. "I am unable at this time to entertain any other idea than Timmy's recovery, and now I shall pray for that."

Her mother sighed deeply.

"Let us all pray for Timmy," she said.

"Yes," the Reverend Stirlington intoned in a deep melodic meditative voice that rang out through the warm spring air as if he was chanting a psalm. "Let us pray for Timmy, and pray that the medicine will cure him, with God's grace and love."

"Let us pray for Timmy," echoed Agnes, and Prudence, and little William.

Timmy lay in bed asleep in his room on the second floor, in the north-east corner of the house, the room with the ceiling entry to the attic. He had been sleeping for two weeks. Breena, the Lady's Maid, sat in a chair watching him and praying. He was visited by his eldest sister and his mother throughout the day and night, they took it in turns to sit by his bedside, they kept watch and prayed. Timmy did not wake. Agnes did not sleep.

Mrs Stirlington had announced she thought it would be beneficial for the Reverend Stirlington and the family to have breakfast together this morning, to try to comport themselves as if all was well, then perhaps it would be. God might again bestow his full gift of love and life, and they would ascend the stairs to Timmy's room, and find him sitting up in bed, smiling, and saying that he was hungry, how long had he slept?

Only two weeks earlier, Timmy had been playing in the rose garden, in the walled garden, near the well, awaiting Mr Quinn who had been called away by Breena, about a delivery by mail coach. Breena walked outside and found Mr Quinn and Master Timmy and asked if Mr Quinn could help her as the Reverend Stirlington was at church and the Lady of the House had gone visiting in the carriage with Miss Agnes and Master William. Timmy said he would wait for his tutor sitting on the stone bench, learning his Latin. The sun radiated warmth and hope, it was a fine spring day.

Mr Quinn was away for rather a long time.

As he sat on the cold stone bench, Timmy had glanced over at the old well that no one was allowed to use. It was covered with a metal lid; and above the font-like structure, atop two plinths at either side, was an arched roof with slate tiles. Some distance away, at the end of the garden, was the pump where the maids pumped up water from the spring that the Stirlington family and their servants drank, and the Stirlington family used for washing inside.

The maids carried spring water to the house in jugs throughout the day and heated it in large coppers on the kitchen stove that was fuelled by turf. The hot water was carried up to the bathroom, where it was poured into a copper bathtub for the family to bathe in, in turn. The servants bathed outside, with pails of water that they threw into the field behind the barn, or they went down to the river and washed there, even in winter.

Everyone said the old well was ancient, but no one could say how long it had been there. Timmy walked through the rose garden and around the well; as he walked he tapped his wooden ball with his cane, aiming at targets that he attempted to hit with the ball. He aimed at a stone near the foot of the well font. As he did so, he noticed that, oddly, the lid was out of kilter, there was a crack through which he felt a draught, a gust of cold air blew out from inside the well.

Timmy thought it very odd that a cold mean wind should be emanating from the well, and wondered was he imagining it. To test it, he walked up and slipped his hand through the small gap; yes, it was cold. He pulled back his hand and could not get it out. The lid was heavy, he could not move it.

Where was Mr Quinn, why was he taking so long?

Desperately, Timmy twisted his hand this way and that, and pushed his arm further into the well space hoping to be able to pull out his hand and could not. His fingertips touched cold slimy stones; the shock made him shiver. Then his fingers dipped into water that made him jump. With an extra twist of his wrist he pulled his hand free. It was dripping.

He skipped to the bench, sat down and, without thinking about what he was doing, absently sucked the tip of his thumb. It smelt like sulphur. He tasted something acrid, almost like a kind of salt.

Timmy realised that his thumb and his whole hand were wet with the well water that no one was supposed to drink.

He felt frightened. He couldn't tell anyone, or he would get into trouble. Suddenly, he felt a blanket was falling over him, wrapping him in a heavy numbing shroud. His head slumped forward, his body sagged, he slid from the bench seat onto the brick-paved path.

Mr Quinn found Timmy there lying on the ground, when he returned from his rendezvous with Breena the Lady's Maid, another secret of that fateful morning.

Mr Quinn said he had been sitting with the young master on the bench, as he taught him the intricacies of the Pythagorean theorem when, with no warning, Timothy collapsed into a coma.

The next day, after attending the morning church service, Mrs Stirlington and Agnes were driven home by the groom. The service had been a mayhem followed by emotional outpourings, confessions and conversions, that would continue with breaks all day into the night, until the Reverend Stirlington, his eyes bleary behind his spectacles, would break the emotional abnegation, ferry the crowds of remaining converts and would-be converts of the night out, bestow blessings, lock the church door, and return to the manse in his carriage, to eat his supper and sleep. That may be twelve hours away, by the tone of the crowds at the church today, thought Agnes as they trotted down the lane towards the house.

"Any change?" Mrs Stirlington asked her lady's maid, she of the black hair, blue eyes and statuesque figure, clad in a flattering white linen dress and apron.

"No ma'am, nothing," said Breena avoiding her eyes.

"I'll take over now Breena," said Agnes, who was wearing a fine blue linen dress and silk shawl.

"Yes, Miss Agnes," said Breena, keeping her face downcast.

After Mrs Stirlington and Breena left the room, Agnes sat in the chair beside the bed. She had hardly slept for two weeks.

She gazed at her little brother's dear sweet face. His tousled fair hair and pale skin.

She felt tired; overcome by soporific torpor, her eyes closed, and she slipped into sleep, sitting upright on the chair.

Agnes awoke suddenly. She did not know where she was. She realised she must have been asleep. For how long, she did not know. She could just see her brother's sleeping form on his bed, before her, in the fading twilight.

"Timmy," she said. "Timmy, wake up, dear little brother." She reached out to touch his face.

His skin was cold. She held her hand above his mouth. No warm breath exhaled against her skin.

She felt for a pulse in his wrist.

There was nothing. No. No throb of lifeblood.

NOTHING!

"Mummy! Mummy! Mummy!" She screamed.

Agnes was screaming.

Screaming as loud as she could.

Screaming in the dark.

But everything they say about me is untrue.

They don't even have who I am right, let alone their stories of what supposedly happened here, and who we were, or are, as a family.

And here I am trying to help this young girl and her family, who've moved in, but because of the false stories they've been told of the so-called "Ghost," in her mind she's terrified, trying to do imaginary battle with me–me!–to overcome her fear of me, or rather not-me not-me, as I am not the spectre in her mind and nightmares, although I will admit I am spectral.

What's more, in terms of family tree, she's not as much of a "stranger" and outsider around here, as she thinks.

And what's furthermore, I'm not the only one.

There are many of us, who've lived here and returned.

32
AGNES IN MOURNING

After the unspeakable tragedy, Agnes had been put to bed and she stayed there for three days. Her father prepared for her an infusion of valerian and camomile to drink; he administered laudanum for nervous shock, injecting it into her upper arm with a hypodermic needle. On the fourth day, she arose and dressed in her black linen dress. Her mother told her that the funeral would be held the following week.

The house felt sombre; the air heavy. Agnes's bedroom was across the hall from Timmy. She could hear the murmuring of voices, her father and mother and others, going in and out of Timmy's room. Her mother said Agnes was not allowed in. To make sure access was prohibited to those not permitted, the door was locked with a brass key.

Yesterday evening, after Agnes had been administered her medicine, unusually she had been unable to sleep. As the day's light waned, feeling ethereal and wraithlike, she arose, quietly opened her door, and glided across the hall, with its patterned rug over wooden boards, to Timmy's door. She felt as if she were floating. She did not know why she had gone there, after her mother had told her not to. But she could not stay away. She wanted desperately to see Timmy, to be with Timmy, for Timmy to open his eyes and look at her and smile.

She turned the door handle. Or tried to. She tried again. The door moved, rattling in the door frame but it would not turn. Locked out. She had turned, noiselessly, and floated over her carpet and into her bed.

Every evening the Reverend Stirlington ascended the stairs to attend to his daughter, and to matters concerning his son, still lying in his room, in his eternal sleep.

That evening, Agnes was pale and withdrawn, lying on her carved wooden bed.

"How are you, my dear child?"

"I have a terrible ache in my head, dear father."

"I will give you some more medicine, and that should help your pain, my dear. I will need to inject the tincture into your arm again, my dear."

After her father completed his ministration with a prayer, he bid Agnes goodnight, and left her room, closing the door. She could hear a door being opened on the far side of the hall.

As she listened to her father gently close that door, she did not hear the sound of the key turning in the lock.

Instead, she heard the audible sigh emitted by her father, and the tread of his footsteps crossing the hall. She heard him lighting the oil lamps on the wall outside her bedroom in the hall, and his receding footsteps as he descended the stairs.

Agnes's ears strained to catch every tiny loose wisp of sound, every creak and sigh. She could hear nothing from downstairs, where her parents' rooms were.

Her governess who'd had a room next to Agnes's had gone away until after the funeral. Mr Quinn had been dismissed.

She was alone on the top floor, with Timmy.

Agnes lay in her bed, listening. She was almost certain that she had not heard her father turn the key in the lock on Timmy's door. It was dark. Suddenly she was overcome by an urge she could not repress. The laudanum made her feel removed from the world, and she could not obey her mother's words as she ordinarily would. She could not remember what mother had said. All she could think about was her overpowering desire to see Timmy, and for him to open his eyes and look at her and smile, and for her to lean over and kiss his dear cheek, his dear forehead and tell him how much she loved him and reassure him that he was going to get better and tomorrow they would play together in the rose garden, throwing balls into a hoop that the blacksmith had attached to the stone wall for them.

She sat up, swung her legs over the side of her bed, and in her white nightgown, with her hair in loose braids, she tiptoed silently across the Manchurian carpet and opened her door. As she crossed the hall she felt as if she was levitating through the golden lamplight.

She reached Timmy's door. Reaching out she put her hand on the handle, turned it, then pushed the door inwards.

It opened.

Silently, she floated into her little brother's room. She could see him, stretched out on his bed.

She glided towards him, and kissed his forehead, his cheek. Then stood back a little way from his bed.

She gazed at him; he looked as if he was sleeping deeply and peacefully.

She gazed she knew not how long.

And then she was back in her bed, in her room. She told no one of what had happened. When she thought of it she trembled. She had a strange feeling, as if it had happened before. Or that none of it had. But the terrible truth that could not be doubted always came back with force. Her beloved brother had left this earth and was with God. That was terrible for her, but it was God's will, her father said, and she should not doubt it, nor think it not right.

That was very difficult.

It would never leave. It would keep returning. The terrible reality would haunt her forever. It would return over-and-over again, what she could never forget.

Timmy was gone. He was her dear, sweet brother, and he was gone.

She returned to her room; lay on her bed. She felt tired and cold. Her brow clammy with sweat, exhausted and shivering, she fell into a feverish sleep.

She could hear Timmy's voice calling her from far away. Other voices. Distant laughing, screaming voices. Whispering. Then, loud and clear.

A girl's voice.

PART THREE

ROXY ZAZA

Ireland. Northern Ireland. England
1974-1975

33

ROAD TRIP TO THE ISLE OF INIS MÓR

Holiday Weekend, May 1975

"Inis Mór?" I asked.

"It's the largest of the three Aran Islands, off the West Coast of Ireland, the Galway Coast." Dad replied.

He had arranged a weekend road trip for the bank holiday weekend and announced this a week or so after I had started the Serendium. I did not register much what he was saying.

When the appointed weekend came, we set off in the rental van. We left on Saturday morning and Dad drove the family south to the border. (We'd left Dusty with plentiful food and water in a stable, and left bowls of cat biscuits and water in the stable yard for Jester and the yard cats).

There was a tense crossing. It made me apprehensive. As we approached the army checkpoint, Dad slowed down; soldiers bearing guns stepped out onto the country lane, waving their weapons with outstretched arms. Dad stopped the van, took out his wallet with his driver's license and passport, and wound down his side window.

Everyone else in the rental van (the same one) was silent. Me, Alex, Lily and Sarah sat sharing the seat belts in the middle seat. Mum in the passenger seat next to Dad. A soldier took Dad's ID and was looking at it carefully. "Could you step out of the van, please sir," he asked.

Dad and the soldier stood not far away from the van, Dad answering questions. As another soldier walked slowly around the van peering through all the windows. I stared ahead. After what seemed like a worryingly long time the solider handed Dad back his ID. Dad walked to the van and climbed into the driver's seat. "Drive on," a soldier said, tapping the roof of the van and waving us through. Dad turned the ignition key.

The soldiers on the road stepped back. On country roads, there were random checkpoints where all vehicles had to stop. This was the first time we had crossed the border here.

"We're not actually going to the South. We're going to the West," I said.

There was some banter amongst us as to whether the West could be called the South.

I sat in the front between my parents, to have a good view of the countryside we were driving through. Sharing Mum's seatbelt. But as Dad drove on, I was scared that we were going too fast. I touched the throbbing pulse point at the base of my throat, panicking.

"Have you taken your pills today?" asked Mum.

"Yes." I felt as if I could hardly see.

I rubbed my left shoulder and gazed through the window; we were driving across a peat bog. Past lots of yellow flowering gorse bushes that Margy called wins. My eyesight felt blurry.

"Please could you go slower, Dad."

"I'm driving well under the speed limit."

"I know, but please could you go a bit slower."

He reduced speed. No one said anything.

We drove through the village of Kells.

We drove past the ruins of a castle in a village called Delvin.

I felt claustrophobic and panicky all the way to Rossaveel, in Galway, where we were catching a ferry to the island of Inis Mór. We parked and left the van in a car park near the wharf.

Why couldn't I feel normal? This was unbearable. I registered very little about the crossing, head in a kind of a fog; but still appreciating the wildness of the sea and the island approaching. The ferry crossing did not take too long.

I stepped off the boat onto the island, with the others.

Dad had told us there were a few hundred people living on Inis Mór, they spoke Irish and travelled by pony carts. The island had sacred sites and an ancient fort, and it was reputed to be a place of healing. I wonder now if that is why he wanted to take us there.

Photographs that Dad took showed me in a pony cart, with Mum, Lily, Alex and Sarah. I am wearing a green head scarf that was once Mum's that I folded into a triangle, placed upon my head and tied at the back, so it kept my long hair off my face. A shift top of plain-woven cloth with a maroon seed pattern, and rolled-up jeans, sneakers. I am trying to smile but my expression looks sunken, my black eye not fully healed. The skin around my eye is swollen, faintly tinged with a dark bruise. We travelled by pony cart near a cliff edge and I gazed at the Atlantic ocean waves breaking on rocks below. We visited a sacred site. I watched my siblings running across stone platforms in the grass. Before we left the island, we had refreshments in a cottage tea shop with whitewashed walls and a thatched roof: griddle scones with cups of tea.

Dad bought a brown woollen Aran sweater. Alex and Sarah looked at books. I felt submerged, underwater, not fully there.

I felt faint, disorientated, and anxious. It was as if I was seeing from the inside of a veil. I was glad when we were on the ferry heading back to the mainland. We stayed that night at a bed and breakfast and drove back to The Old Manse the next day.

34

BALLYCASTLE GETAWAYS

In the year before we went to Sweden, Margy and I had made visits to the coastal town not many miles from my house. We had stayed at Margy's Grandma's house on a street in town. We had explored the sandy strand beach, visited a foreshore cafe, and the amusement arcade. We didn't have much saved pocket money, just enough for an ice cream or instant coffee each day (we took home made sandwiches with us for lunch), but we spent our time walking; one morning we hiked to the narrow Carrick-a-Rede rope bridge, which we dared ourselves to walk across, it was strung, nerve-shatteringly high, above the waves, connecting a grass-topped island to the cliff; we walked across the swaying bridge in turn, terrifying ourselves and each other.

It made a change from staying at each other's houses.

Near the fishing harbour we walked past a music pub over-flowing with revellers, the sound of live music spilled out into the street. But we didn't venture inside.

Half Term Holiday, May-June 1975

After our Easter road trip, Margy suggested that she and I, and Lily and Bee, visit Ballycastle during the half term break, this time to stay at the youth hostel, in a large blue house on top of a cliff at the edge of town. Margy and I had visited the youth hostel to have a look around the last time we were staying with her Grandma. We'd been impressed by the communal lounge and dining room which had views across the Moyle Sea. The place had seemed comfortable and friendly, run by an older

160

woman called Mairead, who told us she had been a three-day eventer (dressage, cross-country, show jumping), in her youth, and still rode. I'd warmed to her. We'd stayed there for a night last summer.

"Okay," I said to Margy, "sounds like a good idea."

We decided that Margy and I would catch a midday bus to Ballycastle. Lily and Bee would be driven to the youth hostel, in the early evening, by Bee's mum.

Saturday, 31st May 1975

Margy and I were sitting towards the back of the empty bus. Our backpacks and sleeping bags on the seat behind us. The bus rumbled along country lanes, scraping hedgerows. It was a warm day. The lambs skipping in the fields were now larger and plumper, on the way to becoming fully grown sheep, or dinner. That thought made me feel sick. I had hand-reared orphan lambs; a friend of Mum's brought a horse float half full of wriggling motherless lambs to our place, last year, where we kept them in a stable with the hens. We fed them with bottles of warm milk, which they sucked, mad with joy, smiling, tails wiggling, until they were sturdy enough to return to their farm. I couldn't bear to think about what happened to them after that.

The bus suddenly shuddered to an abrupt stop. In that part of the countryside, bus stops were few and far between. Bus drivers would stop where people flagged the bus. Standing by the side of the lane was a man, with arm outstretched. The man who looked to be in his twenties, with dark hair curling over his collar, sideburns and a moustache, walked up the bus steps. I couldn't hear what was being said up at the front over

161

the chugging roar of the engine, but the man and the driver started to laugh. We were the only passengers. The man walked towards us. Smiling, he swung into the seat in front of us girls.

"Hello girls!" the man said. "That's a couple of good-looking backpacks ye've with ye there! Where are you off to, this afternoon?" His eyes sparkled; his white teeth flashed under his moustache as he smiled.

"We're going to Ballycastle," said Margy.

"Oh, and what's happening there?" he asked, smiling again.

"We're going to stay at the youth hostel," Margy replied.

"The youth hostel, is it? So, are you travelling around?"

"No," Margy laughed. "We live here, don't we, Roxy?" She nudged me.

"Yeah," I said, without much interest.

"We just go there sometimes, to get away from our parents!" Margy laughed again.

On the outskirts of town, the fella stood up.

"This is my stop, girls," he said. "Enjoy your holiday in the youth hostel. Maybe I'll see you around."

"Bye," said Margy. I spoke nary a word and gazed out the window on the opposite side he got off at.

Margy and I disembarked in town, near the Marina.

We walked up the hill road to the youth hostel. It was a steep climb. We stood outside the building in the clean fresh sea air and looked around, down towards the stretch of sandy beach. Beyond the Marina, on the river estuary, the ruins of Bonamargy Friary crumbled in gothic splendour. Further away the headland, Fairhead, defined the coastline.

I looked inland; across the fields, hedgerows, gorse, heather, peat bogs, and occasional house, Knocklayde Mountain rose up against the sky. Off the coast, Rathlin Island shimmered. I could see the coastline of Scotland, glimmering in a haze on the far horizon.

When we had been here before, Mairead gave us a room to ourselves. This time, Mairead told us that we would be sharing with a party of girl students on a school trip, the students were aged twelve. Lily and Bee arrived and with much mirth we girls made up our beds, arranged our minimal belongings in the dormitory and the communal kitchen cupboards, and set about making tea for ourselves: baked beans on toast followed by cheese, biscuits, and apples.

Later that night as I lay in bed, surrounded by the students, I started to feel strange again. One of the girls whimpered slightly in her sleep and perhaps it was these sounds that set it off. I was just drifting into sleep when suddenly it happened again. My heart lurched wildly. I panicked. This was going to be my last–

I was dying! I gasped; I sat up in the lower bunk, clutching at the pulse point in my throat.

"Roxy. What is it?" Margy hissed, from the adjacent bunk.

"It's my heart," I gasped. "I think it's going to stop!"

Margy got out of her bunk and climbed in next to me. She put her arms around me. "You're okay, Roxy, there's nothing wrong, it's okay," she said.

The tone of her voice was soothing, her arms were warm and comforting. The edges of my terror softened. Slowly my breathing normalised. I didn't want to wake up any students with my panic attack. Gradually, with my friend's arms around me, I fell asleep.

It was raining next day, a soft drizzle tumbling from low grey skies. We girls stood outside the youth hostel, surveying our surroundings. The view which yesterday evening seemed endless was now closing in. Billowing clouds rolled, sending sudden columns of rain hurtling into the ocean. The beach was deserted. In the rain and mist, the town dissolved in a wash of blues and greys. The ruins of Bonamargy, which I saw as towers, kept emerging briefly, only to vanish again just as fast in a haze. But the air was warm, and the rain wasn't heavy.

After breakfast of porridge and cups of instant coffee we dug out our umbrellas and set off down the hill into town.

We spent the day walking on the beach, then later hanging out in the amusement arcade and the café where we drank soft drinks. By mid-afternoon, the sky cleared and the sun came out. We returned to the youth hostel and made and ate our tea. After we had eaten, we decided to go out. Despite the Serendium I felt I could walk for miles. We were all wearing sneakers and jeans (me and Margy), cut-off jean shorts (Lily and Bee), and tee shirts and shirts.

We walked down the hill, singing and laughing loudly. Past the amusement arcade, which was locked up and deserted. Past the café which had closed. People were out strolling along the pavement, near the music pub Margy and I had first walked past when we stayed at her Grandma's. Now we gravitated towards the laughter, the high-pitched violin music, people milling outside its door. Again, we didn't go in.

As we all walked past, a dark-haired man swiftly detached himself from the crowd. I recognised him as the man on the bus.

"Hello girls," he caught up with us in a few strides.

"Oh, hello," said Margy, sounding pleasantly surprised.

"Where are you off to now?" he asked.

"We're going for a walk along the beach," said Margy.

"And who are your friends?" he asked.

"I'm Lettuce," said Bee. "And this is Leticia." She gestured extravagantly at Lily.

"Lettuce and Leticia, eh?" he smiled even more widely. Lily held her head high, tossing her red locks back from her face.

Then the man turned and looked at me and Margy. "And what are your names, I don't believe we introduced ourselves when first we met!"

"How did you meet?" Bee demanded rudely. "Who are you anyway?"

"Ladies first," he said, turning my way. Later, I learned that selecting a girl from a group to favour is a known technique of grooming that older men can use to pick up girls.

"I'm Zaza," I said diffidently, but secretly appreciating his attention.

"ZA-ZA!" screamed Bee. "ZHAZHA GABOR!"

"And I'm Margarita," said Margy. "Who are you?"

"MARGARITA!" shouted Bee.

"Elvis," he replied.

"ELVIS!" we all exclaimed.

"The King!" Screamed Bee.

"That is in English. In the fair tongue, my name is Ailbe."

"What are you blathering about?" said Bee.

"In Irish, my dear, the language of the ancients who guard this land, the land we're walking over.

"Could you spell it," asked Lily.

"Yes. A-I-L-B-E. Well girls," he continued after a slight collective pause. "Now we are all introduced, I will say I am very glad to make your acquaintance."

I found myself listening intently despite myself.

"What are you doing here?" Margy asked, following Bee's assertive technique of interrogating the strange man.

"I play at the pub sometimes on Saturday nights," the man said. "I play guitar. I'm a musician, songwriter, and a poet. Now, girls about this walk ye are proposing. Would ye permit me to accompany ye? I'll keep the bogeymen away. After all, I am a local boy, born and bred, and I wouldnae want to think of four fair young lassies such as yesels out walking and getting themselves into trouble on a darkening night such as this!"

"I can't see much trouble, can you Leticia?" Bee said. Bee had switched positions; she was no longer walking next to Lily, but next to Elvis who appeared to have become our escort.

"No!" said Lily. "And the sun hasn't even set! It's still light!"

"Okay, then," said Margy. "That is, if you can keep up with us!"

We girls and Elvis, who seemed to have become our self-appointed escort, walked quickly towards the river estuary. On the far side were the ruins of the friary looking out to the sea, and the beach landward bound by sand dunes topped with reeds, unbound on the seashore by the restless wild suction of the waves.

"We're walking all the way up to the Rock," said Lily.

"Do you know the Rock?" Bee asked. The Rock was a dark monolith which rose out of the sea, at the far end of the beach. At low tide, it was not too far out from the waterline, surrounded by swirling whirlpool eddies of water. We would calculate our advances, timing the waves, jump out, getting soaked, then scramble shrieking and laughing onto its slippery surfaces, scaling its heights. In high tide it was too dangerous a venture to attempt.

"Oh yes, I know the Rock," the man smiled.

"The Rock at the far end of the beach?" said Lily sounding incredulous.

"I bet you haven't tried to jump onto it when the tide's high— we have!" said Bee, her voice rising. "We did this morning!"

"I'm well acquainted with the Rock, girls."

I decided I didn't quite like the way Bee was commandeering the man's attention. He suddenly seemed more interesting.

We reached the estuary of the River Margy; the clear water was shallow, flowing over sand.

As the others jumped onto a sand island then onto the far bank, I held back with Elvis. I was feeling reflective, not at all like screaming and shouting. The others' laughter tore at my ears like the wind.

"Here let me help you," the man said. He jumped onto the sand island and held out his hand. I reached out and took it. I jumped, landing next to him. Now we were teetering, side by side, holding hands on an island in the middle of the estuary. He let go of my hand and jumped onto the bank. Then held out his hand to me. I took his hand, jumped. Landing beside him on the long scratchy dune grass and reeds. I could see the others running way ahead, racing each other up the beach, the wind whipping their hair and clothes.

"What kind of songs do you write?" I asked.

"Love songs," he replied, turning and gazing mournfully at me, but with a twinkle in his eyes.

Elvis and I trailed the others, all the way along the beach, and back, over the estuary and up the hill to the youth hostel. I could see the others open the front door and go inside.

Elvis and I stopped walking near the blue building, on the opposite side of the quiet road, at the edge of a cliff. The man put his fingertips lightly on my shoulders and gazed at me.

"You have beautiful eyes," he said. "But they're sad. Soulful eyes… What's made you sad, Zaza?"

Forget that I hadn't told him my real name. If only he knew the chasm which had opened up, since the Accident. A void that was impossible to describe, an abyss of negation. It made a mockery of pleasant conversations such as this.

"Can I see you tomorrow?" he asked.

I thought for a moment, as the pause widened. "I'm doing things with the others all day," I said finally.

"In the evening, the two us could meet. You're such a pretty girl. I'd like to get to know you. I'd like to find out the mystery that makes your eyes so beautiful."

I glanced at his face, framed by shoulder length black hair. He had warm brown-green eyes, tanned, weather-beaten skin and, of course, his moustache and side burns. He looked quite a bit older than the one boy I'd had a platonic dalliance with, on holiday in Portugal two years ago.

"We could meet outside the music bar at eight pm, there's a grand fiddle band playing, they're friends of mine."

I paused. Elvis seemed warm, and friendly, and convincing. Uncomplicated and straightforward. A love poet. I imagined I could feel a life force, emanating from him reassuringly, magnetically. Attracting me to him. Unconsciously, I sensed from him a feeling of warmth and life–like a fire to sit beside–to melt whatever it was in me that had frozen over on that fateful Easter night, in the van crash in the snow, leaving me out of reach, in my mind, in the snowdrift. Was this what I needed?

I remembered Doctor Lyon's words, which had so shocked my mother, "Does she have a boyfriend?" The question had been spoken in a tone which suggested (to me) that it may be good for me to have a boyfriend. Considering my parents disapproval at the mere mention of a male name in connection to mine (which I'd discovered when I'd had my brief romance) that Doctor Lyons should venture such a question, as if t'were normal, had had an impact on me. Compounding this, my father was a fan of Freud, and I had several times heard him say that to be happy a person needed work and love…

But I was on my own here with the others. I could do what I wanted. It had nothing to do with parents. I felt breezy and hazy in my mind, it was the way the Serendium made me feel.

"Okay," I said, tossing my long hair back from my shoulder suddenly. I gazed across the dark ocean. In the sky above us, the stars of distant galaxies twinkled and glittered. A crescent moon glowed like a promise.

Elvis laughed. "I'll see you tomorrow then, at eight o'clock. Outside the music bar."

He leaned down and kissed me. His moustache pressed the sensitive skin above my upper lip.

"Enjoy your day tomorrow!"

"Bye," I said coolly as I turned and walked across the empty road towards the hostel.

When I reached the front door I turned my head, glanced back, he was still standing there watching me. He waved, then turned and strode swiftly away down the hill.

The next evening I went to the music bar. I walked down the hill with the others giggling and giving advice along the lines of Bee's "Don't do what I wouldn't do–get my drift, eh Zaza?"

When we saw the dark figure standing outside the door of the pub, the others took a right turn into the town, joking and laughing, leaving me to walk on towards the pub.

"Good evening, my fair lady," he said stepping forwards to

greet me. He was wearing jeans and a tweed jacket over a black satin shirt. I suppressed a chuckle.

Elvis escorted me inside. We found a table with a couple of spare seats and sat down.

"What would you like to drink?" he asked.

"Vodka and orange." Galactic Voyagers were playing a rock and traditional folk fusion, loudly. I couldn't hear Elvis. But I smiled as if I understood. It was only after the band finished their last set that we could talk to each other.

"How old are you?" he asked.

This was a question fraught with layered meanings. Not as extreme as "What are you," but fraught enough.

"How old are you? You tell me, then I'll tell you!" I replied.

"Twenty-five," he said brightly.

I recoiled. But I didn't care, I told myself. I didn't think of him romantically. It was part of the effect of the tranquilizer.

"How old do you think I am?" I asked.

"Eighteen?" His warm eyes twinkled optimistically.

If it wasn't for the Serendium, I might have upped my age. Margy and I claimed we were eighteen when we were actually fifteen and went out to a party at Mulligans' hotel disco, the two of us dressed up in satin skirts, halter neck tops, platform shoes and our purple jackets, escorted by Sherry. But under the effect of the tranquilizer, I couldn't be bothered with pretence.

"Fifteen," I said.

The man spluttered slightly into his beer.

"Fifteen!" he exclaimed. "I almost believed you there!" he laughed.

"No, I am. Almost sixteen." I replied, starting to feel bored.

"Are you serious?"

I didn't reply.

"Well, you're very advanced for your age, Zaza," he said.

"My name's Roxy. We told you made up names."

"Right you are. Roxy then. Now would you like to go for a wee walk?"

"Where to?"

"We could take a stroll along the beach, if you'd like."

"Okay."

I followed Elvis out through the crowds of raucous drinkers. I'd had one vodka and felt woozy and relaxed.

We jumped across the estuary, via the sand island again.

We walked along the beach next to plunging white horses rearing, pawing their hooves and shaking their manes across the ocean. Salty sea spray flecked my face, the wind whipped my hair, I carried my platform shoes, bare toes pressing into the damp sand. My jeans rolled up. High tide wavelets rushed over my cold ankles. Elvis steered a course up from the beach towards the ruined friary. It was dark now.

"Bonamargy, the Friary of Third Order Franciscans," he said. "Let's see if the ghost of the black nun is out tonight…"

"The ghost of what?" I asked.

"The black nun. As she's known around these parts."

"Who was she?"

"Part of the family who built the friary. It's said she moved into the friary after the last friars had left. She lived here on her own until she was murdered." He strode dramatically across a space surrounded by ruined walls.

"Right here…" he ran and jumped, "This is where she met her sorry end, on these very steps, my lady!"

"Murdered? Really?" I said, interested despite myself. It felt like a long time since I'd been interested in anything.

"Indeed. And …" He jumped from the small flight of stone

steps. "This is her gravestone." He bounded towards a circle of stone with a hole in the centre.

"You don't say! And who did you say she was she, this black nun?"

"Well, my dear, the friary was built around the late 1400s. In those days it would have been a fine-looking structure with a thatched roof. The very latest in fifteenth century friaries." I looked upwards past the ruined stone walls and the nave into the clear night sky filled with stars.

"You couldn't see comets at dinner time then, my dear. The Friary was the home of the Franciscans who arrived in Ireland in the thirteenth century. They did well, despite minor adverse factors such as war, and the Black Death otherwise known as the plague. The Black Nun's ancestors are said to have founded the Friary in order to give the Franciscans a base in Ballycastle. But it was taken from them in a battle in 1558…"

I was finding this account, although interesting, somewhat confusing. "But what about the Franciscan friars?"

"They took up residence. It's said they were given the friary as a reward for their missionary work in Scotland. For a while, there were only twelve Catholic priests in all of Scotland, it's said. The Friary was a refuge for Catholics and is said to have been a base for conversions back to Catholicism."

I didn't say anything. It was the old topic. Religion. It went back a long way. I trod carefully as I followed Elvis, through the towering ruins, across the spongy grass.

"In the nineteenth century, long after the friary was ruined, a locked chest was found in this chimney," Elvis said, gesturing towards the remains of a free-standing chimney. "But before it could be publicly opened, it disappeared and no one knows what was inside it, or what happened to it! Then another chest was found hidden in a chimney, and inside it were writings by Thomas Aquinas!"

"But what about the Black Nun? What was she doing here, living alone?" The idea of a locked chest that disappeared was interesting and so were the writings of Thomas Aquinas, but I wanted to know about the mysterious female.

"'Tis said she was a witch, and she had the power of second sight. She was accredited with predicting many events, some of which have come true and some of which are still to come true."

"Like what?"

"Well, my dear, I believe she predicted that a moustachioed musician, descended from a chieftain, would meet a beautiful young girl called Roxy and they would walk together through the ruins of the Friary by the stormy sea, together."

"Come on, let's go back–it's a bit spooky here!" I smiled and turned to walk back. Elvis followed me. He walked with me back up the steep hill to the youth hostel where he kissed me lightly on the lips. We arranged to meet again next day, for another walk.

"I'd like to show you my country, my land," he said, gazing soulfully into my eyes before we parted. "I'd like to take you walking. Do you like walking?"

"Yes," I said. "But I'd better go! I'll be locked out!" One of the things Margy and I liked about the youth hostel and Mairead was that she trusted us to let ourselves in and out, there were no rules that I recall about the time the front door was locked at night. The latest I came back was after ten pm, and the door was still open. She lived in the house and maybe she locked the door at ten-thirty. Anyway, if I had missed lock out time, if there was one, I could have gone around to the back of the building, knocked on the window of our room, and Margy would have opened the window. But I didn't ever have to do that. I didn't want to stay out any later.

I could think of no reason to stop my history and mythology fieldwork lessons with Elvis over the next days. Nothing took my mind away from my existential anxieties more effectively than a brisk walk with my knowledgeable guide. As we walked for miles along cliff tops, in between quoting poetry Elvis told me folklore and myths of the land he clearly loved with a passion.

We walked past a windswept tree in the middle of a field. "Do you know what that tree is?" he asked.

"No, what is it?

"Sceach gheal. It's a whitethorn tree,"

"I've never heard of that."

"It's also called a hawthorn tree. It's been called other things, the gentle bush, the lone thorn. It's also called something else, but people didn't like to say it, in the past."

"What are you talking about?"

"Have you heard of the faerie tree? No. Well people didn't like to say it by name, as it was considered disrespectful to the faeries, and that meant bad luck to whoever mentioned that name; they could be called the wee folk or the other crowd."

I looked at the tree with more intensity.

"It's no different now. Farmers don't like to cut them down. That's why you see them standing like that one out there, on its own in the middle of a field. It's supposed to be bad luck to cut them down, or to cut off their branches, or hang things on them—except at Beltane when it's the custom."

"What's Beltane?"

"The first of May."

"May Day, that's a traditional celebration in England too. There used to be May poles, with long streamers that people held and danced around."

Elvis said that faeries were said to live in hawthorn bushes, and there were many stories of bad luck befalling anyone who cut them down. "If you trim branches from a hawthorn tree, you have to leave out honey to appease the faeries," he said.

I wasn't sure if he was being serious and assumed he wasn't. I smiled. "I'll remember that and make sure I do, if the need should ever arise."

On our walk the next day, the King told me more tales about the Sidhe[3] and the wee folk, who lived under the ground in faerie forts, the smooth raised grassy swellings in the land that dotted the countryside, that he pointed out as we walked.

Elvis said in local lore whenever things went wrong such as milk souring, or butter curdling in the churn, people would blame it on the Sidhe. If babies or children disappeared 'twas said they were taken by the Sidhe. The Sidhe are always on the lookout for human company, and human lovers. They prefer young and beautiful people.

"But do nae worry, I'll protect you," said Elvis.

We kissed on a hilltop with the fields spread out beneath us in hazy green disarray. The King's hands wandered lightly over and under my top, but I did not mind much. (Or I convinced myself I didn't, under the influence of the tranquilizer).

On my last day at the youth hostel, I went on a long walk

---

3   **Sidhe** (pronounced shee) supernatural race in Celtic my-thology comparable to faeries or elves which inhabit sidhe mounds leading to faerie forts underground and the Otherworld.

with the King, just the two of us, along the coastline. Outside the youth hostel we said goodbye.

I told him I'd be coming back here with my friends maybe next month. But Elvis was clearly intent on seeing me again.

"May I come and visit you, at your home, sweet lady?" he asked, not for the first time. "I sometimes walk out that way, and I may be hiking through that part of Antrim soon."

"I suppose so," I sighed. I gave him my phone number and he said he would ring.

"Goodbye, my beautiful young lady," he stared soulfully into my eyes. "Thank you for spending such sweet days with me."

I walked back towards the youth hostel, turning to wave at him at the front door. He was standing watching me, and he waved, then turned and walked back down the hill.

"How's the King?" said Bee as I walked into the communal living area.

"Did you have fun with Elvis?" Margy asked.

They were all sitting on the couches, reading books they'd brought with them.

Lily jumped up and walked towards the kitchen. "Coffee, tea or me?" she asked, turning back, hand on hip striking a pose and pursing her lips in a deliberately grotesque pout.

"Yeah, it was okay, good. We just went for another walk." I looked at her.

We packed up our things and checked out after Bee's mum arrived to drive us back to our respective houses.

A few evenings later the King rang me at home. He was taking a long walk through County Antrim on Saturday, heading my way, could he visit me at The Old Manse in the afternoon at about two pm? Rather hesitantly, I agreed. The idea of Elvis visiting me at The Old Manse seemed odd. But then, so in a way, did everything.

Nonetheless, when Saturday came, I dressed in one of my favourite outfits, my green loons and a purple and black tank top. I brushed my hair without a feeling of total dread, for the first time in ages. Feeling more normal whatever that was. My family went out after lunch to visit a work friend of Father's, leaving me alone. I knew they were going out or I would not have let Elvis visit me that day. I didn't mention to my family that he might be dropping by.

The house was empty. The smiling woman who lived nearby in one of the post-war cottages who came in once a week to help Mum clean and who sat around eating homemade cakes and biscuits, as Mum did the cleaning whilst talking nonstop to her, had been the previous day. (I joked to Margy that Mum was paying her for a kind of therapy to assuage Mum's guilt at hiring a cleaning person in the first place). The house was emanating film star chic, as it did when tidy, as opposed to the film star grunge it manifested when it was untidy (which was when Dad had been away for work for an extended length). But why should I care what the house looked like? And then there was a ring on the doorbell.

"Hello," said Elvis, walking into the hallway. "This is some place you have here."

He looked around quickly, at the hallway and the aquarium set into a rectangular space cut into the wall. Shortly after we moved in, for reasons we couldn't fathom, all the fish died. Dad had emptied the fish tank and Alex had put a miniature cactus from his collection onto the coloured pebbles. I added a few cowboys and horses from the toy box.

"I like your fish," said Elvis.

"Come into the kitchen," I said.

Dad had undertaken renovations at the back of the house, where there had been the 'mud room'. To get to the kitchen you'd had to walk through the mud room, and outside into the stable yard, then back in through the kitchen door. Dad hired a builder to convert the mud room into an open plan dining area panelled with pale pine planks. The floors were polished boards. On the walls hung candle holders Dad brought back from a trip to South America. Now the dining area joined the kitchen; the repositioned back door opened from it into the stable yard. I thought this was the nicest part of the house. It was light, bright, modern and airy.

I offered the King home-made fare: oatmeal biscuits, sticky gingerbread, or soda bread from the tins in the cupboards. He chose a biscuit.

Silently adding up the calories, I helped myself to a golden delicious apple.

We stood together in the kitchen, eating. After staying an hour or so he bade me goodbye.

"I'll ring you soon," Elvis said.

I stood at the front door and watched him walk away down the drive until his striding figure was obscured by the rhododendron bushes. Then I closed the door.

35

WE KEPT ON WALKING

We kept on walking, Elvis and I, step after step, the rhythm of our feet, legs and breathing, interspersed with the fluttering of the tiny blue butterflies. High white clouds raced us overhead, sunlight on the sea glinted silver-gold as we rambled along a cliff top.

After a while of tramping along, we lay down in a steep-sided grassy hollow, the ocean waves rolling and pounding against the rocks at the foot of the cliff below.

The King and I lay on our backs, in my ears rang the mad high cries of the seagulls wheeling and gliding overhead.

Suddenly I remembered.

I sat up and rummaged in my bag, found the bottle, shook out a pill, and washed it down with a large sip of water from my water flask.

"What's that?" Elvis asked, suddenly sounding very serious.

"Serendium." I said vaguely.

"Serendium!" He sounded shocked. "Why are you taking that?"

"It was prescribed by my doctor."

"How often do you take it?"

"Three times a day."

"*Three times a day!*" He sounded even more shocked.

"And how long have you been taking Serendium?"

I did a rather fuzzy calculation. "Two months."

"Two months! You have to stop taking it!"

"I can't."

"You can't? Why not?"

"The doctor said I have to keep taking it, every day."

"Nonsense. They don't always know what they're talking about. These things are not good for you. Why were you prescribed Serendium?" he asked in a concerned tone.

I was surprised by his interest. He was the first person who had asked me about the tranquilizers. I had grown used to taking the pills three times a day now. It had become rather a reassuring routine.

"I was in a road accident, a car crash. Or rather a van crash. With my family on holiday, in Sweden last Easter in a blizzard at night. We almost crashed into a frozen lake; we just missed it and landed in a snowdrift. It was a miracle." I told him the story.

"But the Serendium takes the edge of it all," I confided.

"What a terrible thing for you to go through, but listen to me, Roxy. The pills are no good. And you don't need to worry about your heart, darlin'. The same thing happened to me," said the King.

"What—you were in a van crash like that in Sweden?" I was incredulous and could scarcely keep the scorn from my voice.

"No. A similar thing happened to me with my heart. I could feel every heartbeat and thought I was about to die. I thought I was about to have a heart attack," he said ruefully.

"Really?" It sounded so improbable I could scarcely believe him.

"Yes. It was after I had been taking drugs. I wouldn't touch any drugs, ever again," he said hurriedly. "I went to my doctor, he did tests. He said it was just an after-effect of taking drugs, and that there was nothing wrong with me. If I had a healthy lifestyle, I'd be fine. That's when I stopped forever."

"You have to throw the Serendium away, Roxanne. You've got to stop taking it. Promise me now, my sweet flower." He cupped my chin in his hand and turned my face towards him.

Sitting there with Elvis, I almost felt as if we were in a film and I imagined I could see myself sitting on the cliff top, with him. In the background, the breakers crashed, seagulls wheeled overhead. I could see the scene in a detached distanced surreal way.

"You're fine darlin', there's nothing wrong with your heart, your doctor's told you. Promise me, you'll throw away those pills and never take any more."

I was silent.

"Promise me, Roxy."

"Okay."

That afternoon, on the way home in the bus I thought about what Elvis had said. It seemed incredible to me that anyone else could have experienced the thing I had. It was so far off the map of experience usually talked about at home, at school, amongst my friends.

And for me to have met, and be going out with, someone who said he understood what I had been going through, who claimed to have gone through something with similar effects himself, seemed the most extraordinary coincidence.

Life was an adventure, a journey, and a mystery. You never knew who you were going to meet, or why. The role significant people play in our lives only becomes apparent in retrospect. I had been drawn to Elvis by an attraction which now seemed complex and layered.

That evening I felt calm and peaceful, pleasantly tired after my walk. Thoughtful and reflective too, turning over in my mind what Elvis had said.

I ate dinner with the family.

"What did you do in Ballycastle?" Lily asked.

"I went for a walk," I spooned soup from the edge of my soup bowl.

"How's the King?" Lily asked slyly.

"He's alright," I replied, kicking her under the table.

"Ouch! What was that? Someone kicked me!" Lily wailed.

"Roxanne. Lily. Please, we're eating," Mum remonstrated.

After dinner I went out to the stables.

I unbolted Phoenix's stable door. My horse was standing on straw, head drooping. I edged around his hind legs. I had to be careful with Phoenix. Much as I loved him, and his beauty, he was no docile pony. He could lay back his ears and kick out without warning.

"Good boy," I said. I didn't know why I felt like going into the stable. I just felt like saying a few words to him, feeling his wild, furry, animal warmth. I reached out my hand. My horse immediately flinched.

Now Phoenix was arching his back hoof rather menacingly against the concrete stable floor.

This wasn't working out as I had hoped. Phoenix valued his space and did not appreciate intruders, even his loving owner. It was a secret source of frustration to me that my relationship with my horse did not more closely resemble the relationships the girls had with their ponies in the story books I had grown up reading in England. Phoenix must have been treated badly earlier in his life, and no matter how kind I was to him, he did not much like humans. Poor Phoenix.

I left the stable feeling irritated and anxious, but I didn't swallow my pill that night. I took Elvis's advice to heart. I was tired of the non-feeling, the numbness which had shrouded my thoughts and emotions for what seemed like ages. I wanted to feel like myself. My old self. I wanted to feel emotions again. I wanted to feel something more, something unknown, that called to me deep in my bones. I wanted to feel fully alive, not buried in a snowdrift of non-feeling in a life–my life–that I could only view from a long distance.

I usually followed breakfast with Serendium washed down with coffee. But, next morning, I simply stood up resolutely, walked into the kitchen and washed my bowl and spoon in the sink. I went to school. I felt okay. A little faint but I could cope.

I wanted to see the King again, though I didn't 'love' him. His reassurances, his concern, had reached me. He was the only person I'd spoken to about my 'condition' who made me feel deeply reassured. He had told me that what I was going through was not totally weird but that others had experienced such things too. That made me feel quite a lot better.

36
A SOLITARY WALK ON THE MOSS

One afternoon I decided to go for a walk. I felt like walking to the moss.

The peat bog started soon after the road turned off and I walked until I reached the part that my father rented, which was set a way off from the road. As I walked into the spongy grassy bounciness of moss, the peat bog with mauve flowering heather, yellow flowered gorse bushes–'wins'–and low trees, a cloud of orange and yellow moths fluttered up around my knees. There are fourteen hundred species of moths that live in the environment and ecosystem of peat bogs, I had read. A lot. As well as moths flying around, it was alive with insects, beetles, and dragonflies; in the dark pools, frogs croaked. The drumming of a snipe's wings shook the air; skylarks flew past, and in the distance a hen harrier, hovering, scoured the peat bog below for prey.

The moss was a flowering garden. Teeming with wild-life and plant life. I walked past 'our' part of the moss, looking at the bank that Dad sliced turf from that had smouldered in the fireplace when my parents had Dad's colleagues over for dinner in winter.

I walked on, skirting around the heather bushes. A light wind blew my hair and I found myself smiling at just being there. I reached a large, lichened rock, at the edge of a pool, fringed with reeds, and grasses, spongy with sphagnum moss. By the rock were the remains of trunks of very old dead trees in the pool, some sticking up from the peaty ground next to it.

After sitting down on the rock, I picked up a small broken branch lying near my foot and poked at the spongy ground around the black logs. Something flashed and gleamed in the water. Was it my eyes playing tricks on me?

I blinked and opened my eyes wide. I poked into the ground again and the tip of the stick connected with a hard object. I saw a bright flash, like flames, I closed my eyes. When I opened my eyes again, I still saw a gleam in the moss. I bent to look more closely.

Something metallic was catching the light. I reached out and touched it. A shock rushed up through my fingers and arm. My fingers closed over the object, and I pulled it out of the moss.

In my hand I held a necklace, a pendant on a chain.

It was solid, quite heavy. Most of it was covered in mud, but part of it was washed clear by the water, and that was what caught the light, and attracted my eyes, gleaming and flashing.

I leaned forward and dipped the pendant and chain in the pool, I swirled it around gently, trying to clean off the mud.

Now I could see that it was a gold necklace chain, there was a design engraved on the circular beaten gold pendant. Fine lines in zigzag patterns radiating in circles, like a sun design. Radiating from a figure with long wavy hair, *a flying goddess* for some reason the words sounded in my mind. On the other side I could make out the shape of an eye. I partially dried the pendant and chain on my long-sleeved tee-shirt. As I did so I glanced down into the black water.

Peat Bog Gardening and The Gardener

After the English village garden,
carefully tended for all the years lived there,
and the allotment on farm side of the main road
where he tended rows of vegetables, tomatoes
that needed bamboo stakes, and marrows that
plumped ripe on the ground, and more,
now father's garden is a peat bog.
He tends the rich brown peat of the
underworld, with an ancient space, and makes
cubes of turf to be burnt in the hearth,
as a change to central heating.
We are more than fortunate that we have
central heating. With our own oil tank.
Yet, he plunges in the sleáne and slices

out the turf, in cubed precision.
It was his decision
to do this, to return us to an ancient
underworld where fires burn out of sight
smouldering for centuries even, maybe
beneath our feet.
As he cuts and turns and foots the turf,
rickles and clamps in ancient shapes
of drying and solidifying at the Moss.
Or the peat bog. That windswept
wilderness is called by either name, here.
A peat bog gardener
of the underworld.
We go to help, but arms are not strong
enough and instead, we walk and see
the strange elusive fairy flames.
Blue flames, will-o'-the wisps from a
deep dark netherworld
beneath our feet.
At night we burn the turf
in the living room hearth.
Blue smoke and the pungent
fragrance of peat, ancient and
evocative, strange,
fills the living room of the old house.
Like violin music from another time.
Another place,
deep buried here.
I go to sleep, blue smoke in my hair.
Lulled by ancient dreams.
A time that is calling me from the other world.

That's been smouldering for centuries,
beneath our feet.

I lifted the necklace up high, slid it over my head and arranged the talisman in the centre of my chest above my heart. I began to walk, and as I did, I felt as if I was flying. At the same time, I thought I could hear roaring waves coming from under the ground. Breaking into a crescendo that I could hear as if it was coming from the dark pools I was walking past.

I heard the high-pitched sweet music of a violin…

The ground rolled beneath my feet, and I felt as if I was surfing; riding waves.

I felt as if I was flying on sound waves back to the house.

I knew that the eye sun necklace was special, and possibly quite old.

But for some reason I did not feel like telling anyone that I had found it. I wanted to wear it, I decided, and would explain how I found it later. I had a feeling I was supposed to find it, that it was for me alone, and it was protecting me. But I mustn't let others know about it yet.

That night I wore the flying goddess necklace to bed. I fell asleep holding it against my chest over my heart.

My dreams were profound and extraordinary, and in them I travelled far in space and time, flying through the night to a new day, but when I awoke, I remembered nothing. Except that I had slept.

I didn't take any more pills that week. I went to school; despite feeling disoriented, I was able to cope with most things. But walking down a corridor one morning, I almost passed out.

Everything went black. I leant against the wall, to stop myself collapsing. Mrs O'Reilly, a brisk teacher with grey hair, pink rouged colouring, and red lipstick, stopped and asked if I was alright.

"I think I'm going to faint," I said.

The teacher took me to the sick room and instructed me to lie down. I spent the rest of the day there dozing.

The next two days I spent at home, resting in bed, listening to an album which Dora had lent to me, rereading contemporary Japanese poetry and reading a novel about a road trip. Then, the next morning, a letter arrived for me. Mum was visiting Mr MacCorrigan, the butcher in Ballymacbride, taking him some eggs. I walked down the stairs to the letterbox in the front door. Among letters addressed to Dad was a cream, cartridge envelope. My name and address were inscribed on it in black fountain pen ink, in a beautiful, elegant hand.

Elvis's message of elaborately worded 'affection and esteem' included lines from a song about travelling. His missive was signed "Your ever respectful Ailbe." On Saturday, I woke early. I dressed in a vintage skirt which Mum had made when she was young. Made of woven light wool, it was coloured a deep forest green with red stripes above the hemline. I wore it with a green tee shirt under a white blouse, black ankle socks and sneakers. I tied a green and cream paisley-pattern headscarf in a bandanna over my hair. I brushed out my long hair under the scarf. Then I put a poetry book, and a notebook and pen into my shoulder bag with a bottle of water and an apple.

After eating my bowl of porridge; replenishing the ponies' water and putting them in the front field, I picked up my bag, slung it over my shoulder. Under my tee shirt was my found necklace, hidden from view.

I said goodbye to Dad in the kitchen and left the house.

I walked to the northern end of the lane to wait for the bus to Ballycastle. It was not a long journey to my destination.

It was a while since my birthday. It seemed hard to believe I was sixteen. It had passed in a blur. My birthday tea with a chocolate cake. Margy came over and stayed the night at our house. Mum gave me a book, so did Lily and Margy. Alex gave me a single I had been wanting. Sarah gave me a drawing of a horse. Dad was away. I hadn't gone to school.

The next momentous event in my life would be moving to Australia.

Dad's new job began in September, but our house had to be sold. So, their plan was that Dad would go on ahead and Mum would stay to sell the house with us kids. This included the less than enviable task of packing up the family's possessions. It meant finding homes for our menagerie of animals. Three ponies, Dusty and Jester, the yard-cats that kept vermin away from the dry feed, chickens, rabbits and guinea pigs.

Dusty and Jester were going to go to Margy's family. New owners had been found for the ponies. A friend of mum's who had horses was taking Phoenix and Crackers. One of the girls in my class was taking Berry. It was like a vacuum cleaner was sucking out all I loved. Dusty, Phoenix... I couldn't bear to think about parting from them.

As for Margy... all my friends... the King... I would have to start again. Yet again. That was a challenging, almost unthinkable, thought.

I gazed out of the bus window. There were animals everywhere. Frolicking, grazing; fields of lambs oblivious to their probable fate, allowed to graze so peaceably, to eat so well, because they were being fattened up for slaughter.

Was it better to live in blissful ignorance, enjoying life as you lived it, or to prepare for your death, the inevitable end, by living in miserable awareness? I silently asked the countryside.

Elvis was waiting for me at the bus stop at the top of the hill. We just set off straight away in the direction of the mountain.

"So, do you know now when you're going to be leaving?" Elvis asked me as we walked down a hot dusty street through the last houses. I noticed a young woman was sunbathing in a back garden, in a bikini top and mini skirt.

"No," I said gazing at the girl, rapidly assessing her torso, the proportions of her figure, the length and colour of her hair, the fashion-ability and individuality of her clothes, and overall level of attractiveness–in comparison to my perception of my attractiveness, which was my unreliable barometer in these matters–and whether-or-not Elvis appeared to have noticed her (no). (How could I have ever thought like that). Then, lifting my eyes to the green fields and woods beyond the houses, I looked towards the steep pine clad slope ahead.

"Dad's going soon. But there's still no buyer for the house so Mum has to stay to sell the house and my siblings and I am staying with her. I've got no idea how long it will be. Maybe before Christmas but who knows?"

We walked until we left the town well behind. Elvis helped me climb over an ancient stile into a meadow which sloped steeply uphill. The hot sun radiated down as we walked. After a while we stopped. I took a bottle of water from my shoulder bag, drank and handed it to Elvis.

He had a few sips. I noticed that his arms, beneath the short sleeves of his black tee shirt, were tanned, muscular, covered in fine dark hairs, through which glistened beads of sweat.

"Shall we lie down, my dear?" he asked, sinking to his knees

"Okay." I sat beside him. Tiny blue butterflies fluttered in clouds above the grass. From this high vantage point, I could see the shining expanse of the sea.

The King lay down with his arms behind his head.

I lay down next to him. He pulled me to him. I lay with my head on his shoulder.

"So, how are you?" he asked. "Have you thrown away those pills?"

"I've taken one or two…"

"That's naughty," he tapped my arm with his index finger. "You've got to stop them altogether."

"I haven't had any for a week," I remonstrated.

"Very good," he said. "Keep it up."

I was feeling warm and took off my blouse, under which was my green tee shirt and the flying goddess necklace under that which I had not told him about.

He turned his head and pulled my face to his. We kissed. I don't think he felt the pendant beneath my clothing.

The King and I lay on our backs in the grass. I looked up into the vast blue sky through which drifted fantastical white cloud islands, in changing formations. Birds sang in the woods close by. The King gently stroked my arm with his fingertips. Bees buzzed. Blue butterflies flitted and danced. I closed my eyes. I felt calm and peaceful. That evening, I wrote a letter to Elvis.

But I didn't send it.

37

LAST DAYS THERE

I was walking past the kitchen after school on my way out to feed the horses that were stabled that day. Mum was cutting up a piece of dead cow on the kitchen bench top. I had heard her rhapsodise like a surgeon: "They're intricate and quite beautiful." She had in the past invited me to look, but I refused.

She stopped me.

"Ah, there you are."

"Yes, Mum?"

"I have something to say to you."

I was immediately alarmed by Mum's serious formal tone.

"It's about going to Australia."

"Yes?" I was even more alarmed. "What is it?"

"Daddy and I have decided that it will be best if you go to Australia with him when he goes."

"What do you mean? He's going this month!"

"Daddy and I have been talking about it," Mum's tone was firm, modulated. I was being told. "We have decided that you will go out to Australia with Daddy."

"But why?" I gasped.

"Well, your principal, has told us that were you not leaving the school anyway, you were going to be expelled."

"Expelled!" I gasped again. "I don't believe it! What for?"

"She said that you didn't seem to fit in, and it wasn't helping your education to stay there any longer."

"Oh, really," I said acidly.

I am sure now that she had not mentioned the van crash and my injury to my teachers. Though it was only much later that I realised this; and that if they had known surely it would have helped me. (I would certainly like to think so). Instead, the head injury black eye I got in the van crash was treated as if it had not happened. I seemed to be the only one of us who had developed post traumatic stress disorder (as it would now be called) from the van crash.

"Daddy has conferences in Germany and in Tokyo. He will go alone. I will drive you, Lily, Alex, and Sarah to London. We'll stay with Aunty Daisy for a couple of days, then you will fly from London to Japan where you will meet Daddy. You will spend a week in Tokyo with Daddy then you'll fly on to Australia, to Canberra."

"But–where will we stay in Canberra?"

"You will be staying in an apartment in a university hall of residence, until Daddy finds somewhere for us all to live."

The smell of decomposing cow innards wafted through the warm kitchen.

"And do I get any say in this matter, might I ask?" I asked.

"No, Daddy and I have decided, it's the best thing to do."

"How long will it be before the rest of you go to Australia?" I could hear my voice rising, hysterically, into a wail.

"We'll go as soon as the house is sold," Mum said. She did not pause in her cutting up of the cow's heart. Dusty lay near her feet and glanced up at me with a sorrowful look.

It wasn't until decades later that she told me the real reason she had decided I had to leave early was that she did not want to have to look after me–with Elvis hanging around me. Fair point. I don't blame her. I was hard work. So I don't know if I even was going to be expelled. I forgot to ask her. To be fair to me, it's all a bit of a blur now, as it was then.

I slowly climbed the stairs on the way to my bedroom. I was

terrified by the prospect of flying. The only time I'd ever flown before was the time when I was little and we'd gone to Australia for a few months with Mum when Dad was in India. As we approached Delhi, the pilot announced the undercarriage had not descended, everyone must prepare for a crash-landing. Mum had her three children under seven to look after, so she asked an unaccompanied woman to look after me. I had to move seats, away from Mum and my siblings. Then, with the planeload of passengers braced against the seats and me vomiting in a sick bag from fear, we landed. It turned out that all that had malfunctioned was the light indicating the under-carriage had descended. That was a miracle, too.

It had left me with a wariness of flying (read terror). And a belief in my destiny as the mysterious determinant of my life and how and when I would pass into another unknown realm, through what is called 'death'.

And now I had to do it alone, next week. Fly to the other side of the world. I'd rather dig. My heart lurched and sped. Palpitations. This was the kind of situation that could give a person heart problems if they didn't already have them.

It was several days since I'd taken a pill. I went to my room, took out the plastic prescription bottle from my shoulder bag. I shook one into my palm, swallowed it, with a large mouthful of water from the glass on my bedside table.

I rang Margy and told her. Margy sounded as shocked as I was that I had to leave. She told me in a subdued tone that her parents were going on a holiday. She said they'd given per-mission for me to stay in her house with her while they were away. I replied that I would have to leave for London to catch my flight to Tokyo before then. (I have to admit it did sound quite jet-setting and exotic). We were quiet as this sank in.

"I won't be able to." The slow drug numbness and removal was pervading every cell now. "But you come and stay with us before I go, you must. Come tomorrow, or today, if you can."

I spoke to the King the next day when he rang me from a phone box. He didn't have a phone.

"You're going–when?" he asked.

"Six days time."

"Oh, darlin'." He sounded shocked and sad.

He asked if he could visit me on the weekend. There would be friends staying with us, arriving tomorrow. Good friends from London. The house would be full, it often was anyway.

"I'll ask Mum," I said.

"Mum," I went into the kitchen, "Can Elvis come and visit on Sunday afternoon?"

"Yes," Mum said. I noticed, horribly, that her hands were dripping blood.

The next few days passed in a whirl. I felt atomised, like an atom or molecule floating around aimlessly in the Petri dish of life. I didn't go to school. Now I knew what I'd suspected, they wanted to get rid of me, probably had done all along.

Aunty Daisy (not a relation; Mum's good friend), Josie and Steven arrived, and the house filled with festivity. Aunty Daisy gave me a medallion of St Anthony. A patron saint of travellers. Thanking her, I put it on. Under it hidden from view was the gold necklace. Mum drove us all to visit the Giant's Causeway in the rental van and we walked across the honeycomb of perpendicular hexagonal basalt columns as Mum told the story of the giant Finn Mac Cool who ran across the water to Scotland throwing down before him the stepping-stones he made from chunks of the coastline that he pulled up with his bare hands, to fight an enemy giant.

The chunks of coast-land that Finn Mac Cool threw down before him according to legend, had turned into the multiple thousands of hexagonal columns all of different heights, like church organ pipes that formed the Giant's Causeway, along the coastline, stretching into the sea. We walked across a small part of it.

In the house, an original dividing wall had been removed to make a room larger. From the original fireplaces on each internal wall had been created a free standing central fireplace. That evening I went into the living room to look for a book of Sanskrit love poetry on the bookshelves. I had the idea to transcribe and send a poem to Elvis but I couldn't find it and gave up the search. I sat down at the edge of the fireplace and contemplated everything that had happened in the last weeks.

I'd had my first real boyfriend lasting longer than a snog at the school disco. But I was secretly quite glad to be leaving Elvis. He was too old for me. Even more remarkably I'd found the gold necklace.

But now a new future was stretching ahead, over which it seemed I had no control. I was looking forward to seeing Elvis next day, but I was glad Elvis and I would not be alone. If I'd stayed I would have had to end it, although I had not thought about it too much, as I didn't need to. (And that had nothing to do with what my mother thought about it, which she had certainly not indicated to me.) I was leaving.

I was pleased to have to be leaving him. I was being carried by my destiny far away, and I would not need to think about the dilemmas going out with him were already raising, again.

I would soon be on my journey, heading into an unknown future. The prospect was scary, it was also (terrifyingly) exciting, waves of adrenalin surged through my nervous system. I felt alive. I was alive.

The day I left was a blur, everyone running around. Dad had already left on his journey to Tokyo. There had been a major change of plan. I was going to be living in Tokyo with Dad for a year before we went to Australia, I'd be going to a long-distance School of the Air. Dad would be travelling for his work, to places in Sweden, and Canberra, then back to Tokyo and Kyoto, and I would go with him. I would have school-work and tests; which I would do when I travelled with Dad on his work trips, and in the places where we would stay. By distance education. It sounded bizarre.

"Roxy! Margy!" Lily shouted from the ground floor. "Five minutes and we've got to go!"

I bolted out of my room. Margy hurried from Lily's room. The two of us met in the middle of the hall, in between the bedrooms. With expressions of sudden anguish, we threw our arms around each other. We hugged as if we couldn't let go, tears dissolving our too-brave faces. Then we wiped away our tears; smiling at each other with unspoken love and looking away, I shook my head ruefully at the finality, enormity (and absurdity) of it all. All of it. Margy did the same, at the same time, again, we mirrored each other. And that made us smile ruefully again. Each dressed in flared jeans, tee shirt, waistcoat and platform shoes.

At the front door, Margy's Dad was waiting. Margy and her Dad took Dusty and Jester with them. All I could say was goodbye. Mum drove myself and my siblings on the first leg of my journey. We drove to Rosslare and caught the overnight car ferry to Liverpool, arriving in London next afternoon. After driving to Durham to visit a relative I had never met nor even heard of before and likely would never meet again. A cousin of my father's who we called Hazel and who had prepared an extravagant home-made afternoon tea for us. Mum wanted us to meet as we were going to the other side of the world, and it felt final, as if we would never return. At the end of July 1975, I stayed one night with Mum and my siblings at Aunty Daisy's house in South London. It was all a blur.

Next morning, the first of August, everywhere on newsagent sandwich boards, on the front pages of all the newspapers was news of another atrocity in Northern Ireland. The ambush and massacre of a very popular band whose minibus was blown up on a country lane near Buskhill in County Down at night after they had played a gig. Three were killed; two were injured. Their minibus had been stopped at a fake checkpoint, the band were ordered out of their minibus onto the side of the road, paramilitaries disguised as British Army soldiers pretended to search their minibus, but were planting an explosive in their minibus which went off prematurely, killing the two assassins who were planting the bomb; as the band had witnessed this, the assassins massacred them: three band members were shot dead, two who were flung into a field by the blast survived by pretending to be dead. The injured survivors, bore witness to the attempt to plant the bomb which after investigations is now widely believed was intended to explode as the band were driving on, designed to kill them and falsely brand the band as "bomb runners," and terrorists. The massacre was also seen as an attack on the live music events in Northern Ireland which had brought young people of all backgrounds and denominations, including Catholic and Protestant, together.

It was too terrible to take in.

Mum drove me, Lily, Alex, and Sarah to Heathrow Airport to say goodbye. They stood waving, looking bemused and sad.

I waved one last time, then turned and walked alone down the departure walkway.

I had a window seat. Thirty-two thousand feet below, the ice flows and snowscapes of the Arctic Circle swirled in frozen loops and whorls like marbled patterns on the front and end pages of old books; I swirled white wine in my glass.

The words to the song about not being afraid to die, drifted through my mind. My fear of flying had abated surprisingly now I was in the plane alone. I'd just been to Alaska. The plane had refuelled at Anchorage. I'd walked around the airport and bought postcards that I planned to write, and send in Tokyo. I was on my way, heading into my future life. To the southern hemisphere, following the sun.

I touched the throb of my heartbeat in the pulse point at the base of my throat. I felt the flying goddess sun necklace next to my skin, under my tee shirt and denim waistcoat. Hidden from view. I was wearing platform shoes. I felt strangely free.

Far below, sunlight turned the ice floes and snow to gold. I reached into my shoulder bag for my postcards and a notebook and pen.

PART FOUR

HARRIET

County Antrim
1798

38

THE BATTLE AND THE JOURNEY
The Battle of Ballynahinch, Summer 1798

I am running to the cottage where we have been hiding from the yeomen since leaving the Colonel's mansion. It's a cottage on his estate, where a family is living. Luke and I hid in with their children, as if we were two more of theirs. Sleeping under the thatched roof. Luke, me, and the children. On mattresses stuffed with straw, our shivering bodies covered in linen offcuts, a girl of sixteen and a boy of twelve. We joined the Uprising. At the battle today I dressed as a boy in linen trews, shirt, brown woven jacket, and boots, cropped hair under a cap, with a pike twice my height. Luke beside me. There were women there on horses, with the men. Women, girls and boys were fighting. A young woman aged nineteen, whose heroic story was told last night in the cottage at the fireside. She was an excellent rider, and she rode with her betrothed and her brother, the three of them, she in a green silk dress, holding a green flag. The Irish reinforcements moving in heard the signal to retreat, it was the English troops blowing their horns, but we, the Irish reinforcements, mistook it for our signal to retreat, I too thought we were being attacked and the masses retreated, leading to defeat.

The young woman and her beloved and her brother were surrounded, the soldiers lifted their swords. She put out her arm to protect her beloved and the soldier cut off her hand.

The young woman's betrothed and her brother would not

leave her, refused to desert her during the retreat and the three of them were captured. They were all three executed. I saw it.

My whole body is bruised yet I cannot feel it now, running over the rough ground. The dogs ahead of me, guiding me. I cannot see the cottage for it is hidden from view behind trees.

If I had my horse I would ride into battle, but I have lost my horse. Lightning was stolen by soldiers when our house was raided, and my parents jailed for publishing news of the risings and political essays, and hiding the leaders of the 1796 rising, when the ships with French troops could not land at Bantry Bay due to the wild storm and so the Irish rebels could not avail of their support and were defeated. Luke and I were staying at the Colonel's house and we continued to stay there until we moved and hid again in the cottage.

People from all walks of life are in the risings and rebellions. United Irishmen. United Irishwomen. Protestant. Catholic. Church of Ireland. Presbyterian. Pagan. Agnostic. Atheist.

All these thoughts flash through my mind as I run, panting, with no tiredness, I am speeding with strength, following the dogs. Devastated, desperate, keening as I run in shock. Luke is not behind me. He has disappeared. Vanished.

It's just me alone. Harriet.

I must keep running. The sun is sinking in the red summer sunset. I am drawing near to the laneway to the cottage, and I hear loud harsh voices and screams. I swerve into the thicket of bushes, and huddle down, out of sight. I tuck myself into a ball, under a bush. The hounds have run on, in the direction of the cottage, and I hope they won't return, and give my hiding place away. With eyes closed I remember last night, sitting by the fireside where they had the kettle on, and making rosehip tea, from water drawn from the well near the back door of the cottage. People say that the water from the well has properties, it helps heal wounds. Makes drinkers strong.

It comes from deep in the earth and far down in the well. It must be drawn up in a bucket by turning a handle that winds the bucket up and down on a rope. The well spring has been there since Ireland was created. Since the days of the powerful Queen Medb whose stories are remembered in the tales people tell each other. Mary, my friend, has been telling us the myths, and her brother Patrick sings ballads of the Rebellion, sung to spread the news so people know what is happening, as well as reading the news in the *Clarion Post*.

"This one's for you, Harriet," he said to me. "To inspire you in battle tomorrow."

He sang a ballad.

Then he sang another he had made up for Luke.

All these happy warm thoughts and memories are pressing against my eyelids, as if I am about to sleep, but I am not, I am awake, as the sky is darkening, my ears are tuned to breaking point with the noises I can hear.

Screams, and rough harsh shouting. And now, hoof beats, horses approaching. "Rent unpaid!" A voice shouts. They have come in an eviction party of yeoman trotting along. Safe for me because dark is falling, I am in the shadows, I can't be seen, I lift my head from the leaves on the ground, peer through the bushes.

I count nine armed men in uniforms, on horseback. They are wearing tall, feathered helmets, red jackets, breeches, long boots. They are armed with pistols and muskets. They passed in a laughing group, their hard loud laughter rent the air, and I felt a terrible chill.

I creep through the bushes. Now I can see the cottage with

thatched roof, as I round the bend in the lane, skulking as I am, and I freeze in horror at what I see before me.

From my vantage point I can see the cottage, the side wall, the front, the back of the cottage, the chicken house outside the back door, and the well with its high roof; with its winding system of handle, wooden bucket, and rope, suspended from a pole above.

Screams. Shouts, cries, rip open the air. Terrified shrieking from children inside the thatched cottage.

The soldiers are laughing, swaggering, taking up their guns.

"Mummy, Mummy, Mummy!"

"Mummy! Mummy!" Mary screams.

"Mummy!" Patrick's voice tears the evening apart.

Little children's voices scream. The baby wails.

And now I see horrific things. A man in uniform, is walking out the door with an infant, he shoots and throws the body in the well. I cover my eyes. Shots shatter the air.

Again, again. Again.

And then a rushing familiar roaring, and smell. Burning.

I feel the heat of a fire.

Open my eyes, see the blaze. At the cottage windows Ma Kilkenny surrounded by children screaming. Beneath burning thatch.

I shut my eyes tight and block my ears with my fingers.

Day's first light reveals a scene of horror.

Charred, blackened stone walls; thatched roof burnt away.

No signs of life.

No blessed children, no family.

Mary's spinning wheel she spun flax on, charred.

Bones. Skulls of humans. Infants.

Unspeakable carnage.

My heart shatters.

And here are the crows, flapping and cawing and screeching around the horrific scene.

I curl up under a bush, shake like the rhododendron leaves in the cold wind that is blowing.

I put my hand to my throat, to my necklace amulet of the sun's beneficence, to give me strength, I did not think of it as I ran. All I was thinking of was running, and Luke.

I cannot feel it.

It is not there.

My amulet is missing.

I remember we were running across the peat bog, I slipped and fell into a pool. My head was under black water. I tried to pull myself into moss around the edge, and then Luke came up looking for me, he helped me scramble onto the bank then together we ran and ran. My sun amulet must have slipped off in the water, maybe the chain broke.

I stayed here to make sure to give the men in uniform time to leave and be off. Before I sought to make my exit. So there'd be none around here left to see and hunt me, or so I hoped.

Now I must run from here.

Try to find my way back, but back to where I know not.

My parents are both in jail. The colonel's house was raided. Luke, my beloved brother.

I know now Luke is no longer with me in person, but he is with me forever in his angel spirit. We will always be together. He is a young warrior who fell nobly fighting for the freedom of our country, and the people, and the higher things.

I set off as day's first light touches the dark green fields with brilliant gold.

I think of brave Betsy Gray, the young woman rider in her dress of green.

Of Queen Medb, and the Morrigan, and Cu Chulainn and Fionn Mac Cool, the stories and ballads I heard in the cottage and in the fields as I helped with picking flax. And, my mind full of mist and a red haze, I walk on, until I disappear.

I want to hear those stories again and I want someone to tell them. But I can't find anyone to tell them to me. I keep walking and walking, and then I walk in a reverse circle and return by chance to the site of the cottage, and in its place is a larger house.

From inside I can hear voices talking, laughing, the warmth of their tones draws me onwards, like the happy warmth of the friendly household that was there, with a fire in the grate, a kettle boiling. My ears strain to catch every echo, every creak and sigh. I am listening for stories, for news and for ballads, for voices to tell and sing me the stories of what's been happening while I've been away. While we've all been away. For so long. Tell me stories from all times, to gladden my heart and make me wonder, and hope it was all worthwhile.

I walk up to the house; like a zephyr through the window, I slip inside. Come on, I say, and Luke who was behind me after all follows me into the house.

CODA

ROXY

Shipwreck Bay
Southwest Coast of Victoria, Australia
2025

39
RETURN
Shipwreck Bay
Spring 2025

I peruse my notebook.

Over the years, I researched the history of the house where I lived in Ireland, and the voices of the girls came to me, telling me their stories, which interwove with mine, by virtue of being there in that place, yet at those different times. I lost my fear of ghosts, of who I was. I wrote those words years ago. I'm an adult now, of course, in my mid-sixties. But I have had a nightmare again of the house and the ghost, following the unspeakable tragedy too terrible to write of. In this house where I live, it returned. If I can release this story, I hope that I might release the inner hold of the nightmare on my life, so it does not return with force, as it did when I was a girl.

I am surrounded by boxes. Every room in this house holds cardboard boxes of things from another place I had to leave so fast. Although I put my valuables in a bag so I could keep these things close, tragedy erased my memory. Everything started to slide. And then the nightmare slipped in from where I knew not. But I do know. From trauma, shock, horror, and grief.

Something unknown guided me to that box in my study. One of dozens that looked identical. I sliced the sealing tape and opened it. There it was, coiled in a blue bowl, not wrapped, nor in a jewellery box. The gold goddess necklace of the sun. Solar power. A thrill of electricity tingled through my nervous system, as happened the first time I saw it, and fished it out of the pool. I reached down; my fingers wrapped around the gold. I picked up the ancient necklace, and touched it to my chest, my face, I held it above my head and slipped it down and around my neck, arranging it in place over my heart.

I thought I had lost it.

Now it has returned itself, and I have found it.

I close my eyes and hold it to my chest. I have the rushing dreamlike sensation I am flying.

As I stand breathing more calmly than I have for weeks, the telephone rings. Just as I am reaching to pick up the handle of the wall phone in the hallway, after hurrying to it, the ringing stops. I walk into the kitchen, pour a glass of water from the tap, take a few sips, gaze out through the window, then return to my desk, and check my emails. This is strange. I reach for the goddess pendant, like a protective talisman. There's a new email from Nature Waves. What do they want, why are they contacting me now after all this time? I click 'open'.

SOS... It's an emergency... to save our souls...
the tidal wave is coming... meet with us this afternoon...

There are details of places, more details. Background...

I close the laptop lid and stand up. Pick up notebook, pen, camera, laptop, slide them into my backpack. Pull on my hat. With my flying goddess necklace on top of, not under my tee shirt, I open the front door–and fly out of the house.

AUTHOR'S NOTE

This is a fiction novel inspired by my experience of living in a reputedly haunted house, an old manse, from the ages twelve to sixteen in County Antrim during the Troubles; and also going on road trip family holidays. The van crash in a blizzard in Sweden is based on my real life experience yet is fictionalised. The distant historical sections are my speculative fictional stories, imagining the lives and deaths of people who might have lived there before. Some names of places are changed; others are not. Some historical incidents mentioned are factual and non-fictional (the Troubles; the Irish Famine; the 1798 Irish Rebellion). The popular band that was massacred on July 31, 1975 was The Miami Showband. Any perceived resemblance of the fictional characters to actual people is unintended and coincidental.

Suggested further reading:

Travers, Stephen and Fetherstonhaugh, Neil. *The Miami Showband Massacre: A survivor's search for the truth.* Frontline Noir, 2018.

Kelly, John. *The Graves are Walking: A History of the Great Irish Famine.* UK: Faber & Faber, 2012; USA: Henry Holt & Co, 2012.

O'Neill, Siobhán. "The Story of the Irish Famine Orphan Girls Shipped to Australia." *The Irish Times* online, Nov 7, 2019.

Kleinman, Sylvie; Clarke, Francis. "Gray, Elizabeth ('Betsy')." *Dictionary of Irish Biography* online, Oct, 2009.

Cain Archive–Conflict and Politics in Northern Ireland. cain.ulster.ac.uk (on the Troubles from 1968).

Acknowledgements

I am grateful to my family and friends for moral support over all the time I was writing this novel, and my thanks especially to Max and Ella, and Andy and Audrey, Paul, Clare, Lucy, the real 'Margy' and the Seven (you know who you are), and Philip, without whom (at various times in different places) I could not have started, written and finished this novel.

I would like to thank Doctor Catherine Cole my former PhD supervisor when I wrote the first draft of this novel for reading my fledgling manuscript when I wrote it twenty one years ago, which now, years later, I have returned to, substantially edited, added to, and rewritten into a finished form entitled *The Girls and the Ghosts of The Old Manse Revisited: An Australian Fugue Novel* and am publishing it for the first time.